RED HERRINGS

TIM HEALD

MACMILLAN

First Published 1985 by
MACMILLAN LONDON LIMITED
*4 Little Essex Street London WC2R 3LF
and Basingstoke
Associated companies in Auckland, Delhi, Dublin,
Gaborone, Hamburg, Harare, Hong Kong,
Johannesburg, Kuala Lumpur, Lagos, Manzini,
Melbourne, Mexico City, Nairobi, New York,
Singapore and Tokyo*

Typeset by
ELECTRONIC VILLAGE LIMITED
Richmond

Printed and bound in Great Britain by
ANCHOR BRENDON LIMITED
Tiptree, Essex

British Library Cataloguing in Publication Data

Heald, Tim
  Red herrings.
  I. Title
  823'.914[F]   PR6058.E167

  ISBN 0–333–39893–9

For Dorothy and Calla

ONE

It was not as sinister as the Caistor Gad Whip nor as anthropomorphic as the Horn Dance of Abbots Bromley; not as business-like as the Lot Meadow Mowing nor as alarming as Punkie Night in South Somerset but the annual Popinjay Clout at Herring St George was nevertheless a very old English custom.

No one knew the origins of the Popinjay Clout, not even old Sir Nimrod Herring whose ancestors had come with the Conqueror. Some said it went back further than the Herrings and that it was something to do with the old Saxon 'fyrd'; others said it originated in the martyrdom of Saint Ethelreda, a virgin milkmaid of the sixth century who had been slain by some drunken villeins and cottars one Friday night; an American academic said that it was part of the Robin Hood legend, which was odd as Herring St George was not in Nottingham. It was all extremely confusing.

The actual ceremony was, however, simplicity itself. At twelve noon all the men of the village, dressed entirely in green, marched to the Great Meadow by the banks of the River Nadder. There they fired arrows from their yew long-bows quite indiscriminately into Gallows Wood. After an hour a halt was called and the village women, in smocks, went into the wood to retrieve whatever had been slaughtered in the bombardment. A kill in the Popinjay Clout was as rare as a score in the Eton Wall Game. Ten years earlier Sir Nimrod himself had bagged a rabbit. There had been nothing since.

This year, the day of the Clout dawned brisk and blue

and bracing. The TV team from Channel 4 and Mr Philip Howard of *The Times* arrived to record the event, as did busloads of tourists, many American. On the command of 'fire' from Sir Nimrod, arrows swooped away towards Gallows Wood, cameras clicked and rolled and Mr Howard's pen raced purplish across the page of his reporter's notebook. It was very quaint and everyone was looking forward to the ale and Bath chaps, the mead *frappé* and chitterlings which were a traditional part of the proceedings.

'A capital Clout!' exclaimed the Reverend Branwell Larch slapping Sir Nimrod boisterously on the shoulder. And indeed it was. The bowmen had shot nobly; the sun had shone; the grass was neatly mown; dog roses adorned the hedgerows and clambered about the immaculately whitewashed thatched cottages; even the smell of silage and chicken droppings which sometimes interfered with rustic charm was subdued for the day. Everything in the garden of England was lovely. Then, suddenly from the heart of Gallows Wood, there came a maiden's shriek.

It would have been a chilling sound wherever and whenever it was uttered but on a midsummer day in rural England in the middle of An Old English Custom it was beyond description. And as the shrill keening was taken up by a chorus of other women, even the purplest face (and Herring St George was usually a sea of purple faces) turned quite white. The stiffest knees trembled and the juttingest jaw sagged. Even Simon Bognor, that apotheosis of phlegm, froze momentarily as his teeth clenched around his first sausage roll of the day.

Seconds later the reason for the feminine distress was made clear. For the first time in a decade there had been a kill in the Popinjay Clout. They had found a Mr Brian Wilmslow leaning against a blasted oak, looking a little as if he were posing for a portrait of Saint Sebastian.

He was, of course, extremely dead.

8

TWO

Simon Bognor and his wife Monica were not natives of Herring St George but they were staying in the village for Clout weekend with their friends Peregrine and Samantha Contractor. Peregrine was a very grand Anglo-Indian Old Etonian whose father had made a fortune in railways. Peregrine had used this fortune to make another one out of mail order lingerie. This was where he had met Samantha. Samantha was the leading model of mail order lingerie in Britain.

It was also lingerie that had brought Simon and Peregrine together. There was something a touch shady about the mail order lingerie enterprise and, as a special investigator of the Board of Trade, Bognor had been charged with finding out what it was.

'Something fishy about this business,' said his boss, Parkinson, in characteristically dour fashion, as he picked his teeth under the smiling portrait of Her Majesty the Queen.

'You mean fish*net*,' said Bognor grinning facetiously. 'Fish*net* stockings. Those sort of silky black mesh things women wear with top hats.' He had had a more than usually good lunch and was feeling over-confident.

Parkinson glowered, and Bognor sighed. He knew it was a feeble joke but something about Parkinson's glum, behind-the-times prissiness invited feeble jokes.

'We both know perfectly well what I mean, Bognor,' said Parkinson, and this was true, as it usually was, so that Bognor had shuffled out still grinning, though now a little ruefully, and gone off to investigate frilly knickers and flimsy bras. He had been able, as he put it to Parkinson, in another ill advised attempt at humour, to uncover nothing at all. He sensed that all was not quite what it should be at Fashions Sous-tous, as Peregrine Contractor called his business, but he was unable to put his finger on it. He also found Contractor highly engaging, especially when he attempted to bribe him with a job lot of frillies and flimsies for Monica (Monica was much too big for them).

Since then the two men had remained acquaintances if not exactly friends. The Bognors had been to the Contractors' box at Ascot and Covent Garden; the Contractors had been to brunch chez Bognor. Bognor was careful not to mention the relationship to Parkinson; but if his flinty superior had found out, then Bognor would have explained that he was keeping an eye on him 'just in case'. 'Just in case' had become one of Bognor's favourite phrases. Enigmatic ambiguities, he had discovered, kept people guessing. Which was essential when one was still only guessing oneself.

Much of Bognor's work at the Board of Trade was based on guesswork. There was, he knew (or rather had been told, which was not the same), a different, more logical way of doing things. Ever since he had first entered the Board of Trade due to that dreadful misunderstanding with the University Appointments Board, he had endured advice from men like Parkinson.

'A more forensic approach on your part, Bognor,' his boss would growl from time to time, 'would do us all the world of good.'

A fearful squirt called Lingard had briefly come to share his office before moving on to higher things. 'I see absolutely no method in your brand of madness,' he would complain, morosely, as Bognor lurched from hunch to hunch. Even the long suffering Monica, Mrs Bognor, would occasionally lecture him on the need for what she called 'ratiocination'. Bognor, despite his honours degree in modern history, had had to go to the dictionary where he found that the word meant you used syllogisms. On looking up 'syllogism' he discovered that it was a 'form of reasoning in which from two given or assumed propositions called the premises and having a common or middle term a third is deduced called the conclusion from which the middle term is absent'.

'Oh, really!' he protested when he digested this. 'Life's not like that. Life's much more complicated.'

'*Au contraire*,' riposted Monica, 'it's only complicated because you make it complicated. If you were logical you'd be better at everything.'

'I'd end up like Hercule Poirot or Miss Marple.'

'You could do worse,' said Monica.

Bognor sulked.

They had been greatly looking forward to the weekend of the Popinjay Clout. There would, the Contractors promised, be excellent food and drink, scintillating company, terribly House and Garden surroundings and the engaging diversion of the Clout itself. Now, on top of all that, there was death.

'Oh, bloody hell,' said Bognor, when the news came through on the Herring St George grapevine. 'This is supposed to be a weekend off.'

'Don't be so insensitive,' said Monica. 'Someone's dead. That's a tragedy not an inconvenience.'

'It may be a tragedy for the corpse and their nearest and dearest but as far as I'm concerned it's thoroughly inconvenient. I was hoping to do a lot of lolling about and eating and drinking. Now I shall have to dust down the syllogisms and ratiocinate.'

'I don't see why,' said Monica with characteristic asperity.

'You wouldn't,' replied Bognor, equally tartly.

'I say.' Peregrine Contractor was wearing very tight Lincoln green drainpipes and a well tailored matching jerkin which almost concealed his natty little paunch. A self designed forage cap with rakish feather over one ear was supposed to create an illusion of Errol Flynn. Not quite successfully. 'Have you heard?' he enquired. He was breathless from excitement and unwonted exercise.

'No,' said Mr and Mrs Bognor. 'What?'

'He's one of yours,' said Mr Contractor. 'The stiff. He's a spook from your neck of the woods. A government inspector no less. Awkward, I should say. Name of Wilmslow. Friend of yours?'

Bognor shrugged. 'The Board of Trade's a huge government department,' he said. 'There may well be a hundred and one Wilmslows lurking in its woodwork. But not one that I know. What's he do?'

'Value Added Tax. He's a VAT inspector.'

'The dreaded VAT men aren't from the Board of Trade, Perry.' Bognor was affronted. 'They're Customs and Excise. Not at all the same thing.'

'Oh.' Peregrine Contractor flapped a hand in limp dismissal of such nitpicking, 'I always imagine all you Whitehall wallahs are in cahoots with each other. What does bring it rather home to one is that he was coming in tomorrow to look at the books. Well he won't be able to do that now.' He laughed. 'I suppose they'll send someone else.'

'What exactly happened?' asked Monica.

'Well, darling, no one knows exactly what happened.' Contractor patronised Monica just as he patronised most women.

'His problem was that he wandered into the woods at the wrong moment. No teddy bears' picnic for him.' And he sang in a disagreeably off-key falsetto. 'If you go down to the woods today, you're sure of a big surprise.'

Bognor brushed sausage roll crumbs from the lapel of his blazer. He was not a blazer person but Monica had insisted he invest in one. Something to do with her parents or her brother-in-law. 'This is a pretty serious business, Perry,' he said. He remembered Monica's criticism of him. 'Someone's dead,' he said. 'Which may seem like a mere inconvenience for many of us. For some people, though, it's a real tragedy and it's my job to get to the bottom of it. If there's a bottom to get to. Accidental death is one thing. Murder is another. What was this?'

'Search me,' said Peregrine. He gesticulated theatrically in the direction of Gallows Wood. 'You could hide an army in there let alone a dashed Value Added Tax inspector. You can't possibly suggest he was shot on purpose. None of the archers could have known he was there.'

'Couldn't they?' Bognor spoke sharply. He was irritated. Contractor seemed to be treating the incident almost as if it was part of the pageantry. Indeed, now that the news had sunk in to the collective consciousness of Herring St George and the audience of tourists, this seemed quite a common reaction. No one showed any sign of going home. There was a pervasive, speculative and frankly excited buzz. Bognor who had seen enough death to regard it as almost routine was, not for the first time, mildly revolted. Still, he had accepted, long ago, that murder was, at least in part, the world's most popular spectator sport.

'Not with you, old shoe,' said Contractor. Contractor habitually referred to Bognor as 'old shoe', an expression he claimed to have picked up at Yale Law School, though Bognor was fairly sure Contractor had never been within miles of Yale. His formal education had ended prematurely when Eton had asked him to leave after an incident involving maids.

'Just because they couldn't see the man,' said Bognor testily, 'doesn't mean that they didn't know he was there.'

Samantha Contractor, who had been scouring the field in search of gossip, now rejoined them. You could tell she was some sort of model on account of her smock which she had designed herself and which was an exceedingly brief piece of linen only just held together by quantities of black leather thong. She did have an extraordinary body and depending on how she bent and moved it was practically all on public display.

'Isn't it all too just perfectly ghastly?' she asked no one

in particular, lisping through shiny purple lips, 'What's going to happen?'

'The Clout must go on,' said Peregrine gravely. He had recently been elected to the Clout committee, a sure sign that he had been accepted into the community. The ten thousand he had, not quite secretly, donated to the church belfry appeal fund, had helped quite a bit. It was a gratifying compensation for being blackballed by White's.

'I've been talking to the man from the fuzz,' said Samantha. 'He's rather dishy. I told him about you Simon, dear, and naturally he's dying to meet you. He's going to come over and have a glass of bubbly when he's done whatever you have to do with the corpse. He seemed to have heard of you.'

'Heard of me?' Bognor bristled.

'I said we had this tremendously super detective staying for the weekend and when I told him your name, he said, "Not *the* Simon Bognor?" So naturally I said "yes".'

Monica snorted. 'I expect they're using your past cases at the police training college,' she said. 'What was his name?'

'Guy,' said Samantha fluttering vast stuck-on eyelashes at an unimpressed Monica. Monica wore virtually no make-up and nothing false. 'Take me as I am' was her attitude, 'Like it or lump it.' She found Samantha preposterous.

'Guy?' she said. 'Is that a surname or a christian name?' Samantha said she didn't know. She said that she had introduced herself as 'Sammy from the manor' and that when she had asked him who he was he had held out a very virile hand, looked her straight in the eyes and said, simply, 'Call me Guy.' Samantha grinned. 'He really is ever so dishy,' she said.

'I do rather wish you hadn't brought me into it.' Bognor, though understandably susceptible to Samantha's body was less than impressed by what passed for her mind. He spoke huffily. 'Sudden death really isn't my pigeon. Codes and ciphers are about as exotic as I get. Mostly it's petty irregularities regarding South African oranges or smuggled mink.'

Samantha pouted. 'But Simon darling,' she said, 'we met you because you were showing a sudden interest in ladies' underwear. You can't say that isn't exotic.'

'It really isn't a joking matter,' said Bognor. 'As you know perfectly well, I am merely a common or garden investigator with the Board of Trade. It is not a job that has any particular glamour. In fact frankly it's not even interesting most of the time. I would much rather do practically anything else in the world, but like most people who are stuck in god awful jobs they don't enjoy, I need the money and I'm too old to change. I'm stuck. Just like most people are stuck. And the last thing I need is to have bloody policemen lumbering me with a lot of silliness just because some damn fool VAT inspector has got himself riddled with arrows while walking in the woods. This is supposed to be a weekend off.'

'Well I'm very sorry I'm sure,' said Samantha. 'I was only trying to help.'

The situation was partially restored by Peregrine. In the smouldering silence that followed this little exchange there sounded the discreet gasp of a champagne bottle blowing its top. Seconds later Samantha's husband emerged from behind the Rolls Royce carrying a tray with an open bottle of Veuve Clicquot and glasses. 'Time for drinkies, boys and girls,' he said.

The champagne not only cooled tempers it also acted as a magnet for those villagers who were not averse to a glass but who would normally have had to stick to something less elegant and less pricey. Home brew even. The first free-loader was the Reverend Branwell Larch. 'The padre's a fearful piss artist,' confided Peregrine to Simon and Monica, the night before. He had predicted that he would be the first to show, so there was no surprise when he arrived looking doleful.

'"That which the palmerworm hath left hath the locust

eaten,"' he said in a sort of conversational plainsong, nasal and thin. He wore a cassock with the air of a man who enjoyed dressing up and had a thin, pink veined face with thin, slicked, black hair. Late forties, Bognor judged.

'And,' said Peregrine Contractor, rather surprisingly, '"that which the locust hath left hath the cankerworm eaten."'

Monica compounded the surprise. '"And that which the cankerworm hath left hath the caterpillar eaten,"' she said, '"Joel, chapter one, verse four."' She raised her glass and stared at it thoughtfully. 'There's a wonderful verse just after which starts off, "Awake, ye drunkards and weep". Very good stuff, Joel.'

'Monica has "A" level scripture,' said Bognor by way of explanation. 'Her convent insisted. She's still very hot on the Bible.'

'It's an extremely good book,' said Monica defensively. 'Full of good things, don't you agree, Vicar?'

The Reverend Larch, gaping somewhat, agreed, and accepted a proffered glass.

'Yes,' he said. 'And as relevant to our modern times as it ever was. The eternal verities remain, ah, how should one say, eternally, well, veritable.' He smiled and then realised rightly that something more was expected of him. 'Very salutary to have death visited on us in such a violent fashion. And on such a lovely day. "In the midst of life we are in death" as the prayer book says. We could have hardly had a more dramatic demonstration of that. So at least some good has come from the wretched fellow's passing. Though one has to concede that God really does move in the most mysterious ways.' The vicar was groping desperately for the thread of his argument. Any thread, any argument. He sipped champagne as a delaying tactic and then said: 'And death in whatever shape or form is uniquely mysterious, don't you agree, Mr Bognor?'

Bognor and Mr Larch had been introduced earlier in the morning. The vicar, who fancied himself as a judge of character, had decided that Bognor was a sympathetic and intelligent person even if not of the faith. Bognor had said something disparaging about monasticism. The line was prompted by the vicar's dress. Bognor had had an aversion to that sort of thing ever since some unnerving experiences in an Anglican friary early in his career, but the vicar knew nothing of this and was in any case not keen on monasticism himself. He believed in getting in among his flock, and was fond of describing himself as 'a people's parson'.

'I've always found death disturbingly straightforward once it happens,' said Bognor. 'It's the events leading up to death which are mysterious.'

'That may be your experience,' said Mr Larch. 'But in my line of work life after death is the ultimate mystery.'

'My husband takes a rather prosaic view of this sort of thing,' said Monica slipping a protective arm through Simon's. 'In fact he takes a prosaic view of almost everything. Don't you, darling? But so would you if you worked for the Board of Trade.'

'In any event,' said Peregrine Contractor, pouring more champagne, 'I'm sure we all agree that it's absolutely tragic. A tragedy for the village, too.' Everyone looked suitably solemn but they were disturbed in this moment of reverent contemplation by the advent of Sir Nimrod Herring and his daughter Naomi. Sir Nimrod, last of the Herrings who had come to the village on the coat tails of the Conqueror, had once lived in the manor, now occupied by the Contractors. New money had, as it always did, driven out old; ancient lineage and immaculate breeding had proved no match for ladies' lingerie. Despite having fallen on hard times, however, the old squire had not moved from the village which had borne his family's name these nine hundred years and more. Forced to trim his cloth and turn an honest penny he had taken over the village post office and there he now presided with Naomi under the legend 'Herring and Daughter'.

He was an amiable seeming person with a white tonsure

and a tuft of hair in the middle of his chin. This, unaccountably, was rust coloured with only a few flecks of grey. His daughter, Naomi, was a round faced woman in her early forties, figure concealed in a smock which was as discreet as Samantha's was not.

'What a perfectly bloody business!' he exclaimed, helping himself to champagne. 'Thank God for something decent to drink after that bloody mead. It doesn't matter how much ice you put in the damned stuff it still tastes of bees' wax.'

'Oh, Daddy!' said Naomi. Naomi was permanently embarrassed by her father and none too bright. After Lady Herring, her mother, died in faintly mysterious circumstances (drowned in the moat) Naomi had gone through a prolonged 'difficult' spell. She had been a hippy among the flower people of Haight Ashbury in the sixties; then returned to ride pillion with a chapter of Hell's Angels from Ruislip before setting off on the road to Katmandu and spending a saucy two years in an ashram in Poona. Latterly she was alleged to have settled down though no one was entirely convinced. She was rumoured to have had a child by one of the Rolling Stones but, if so, no one knew what had happened to it. It was also said that she was devoted to Sir Nimrod and it was certainly true that she put in extremely long hours behind the counter. And she was very decent at coming out late at night to drive the old squire home when he was too tight to do it himself.

'What a silly fellow, wandering into the field of fire during Clout,' said Sir Nimrod, 'asking for trouble. Could have been killed.'

'But he was, Daddy,' said Naomi, eyes very round, face very pale.

'Just as I said, child.' He glanced at Bognor to whom he had not previously been introduced. 'I don't think we've met,' he said, sticking out a hand which Bognor shook, 'Herring.'

'Bognor,' said Bognor, 'and this is my wife Monica.'

'Bognor!' Sir Nimrod's eyes flashed. 'Any relation of old Theo Bognor?'

'Not that I know of,' said Bognor truthfully.

'Old Theo was in my company at Arnhem,' said Sir Nimrod. 'Any friend of his is a friend of mine. So you're no relation. Ah well. Naomi and I were talking about this deuced corpse. He was from the Customs don't you know. A bumfwallah. Come down to sort out everyone's Value Added Tax. Damned waste of taxpayers' money if you ask me. They should be out catching criminals. You should see the pieces of paper we have to deal with in the post office. Licence to breathe is what you'll have to have before you can say knife. I say, Vicar, I thought you'd be over in the woods saying the last rites. Not quaffing the Widow with the nobs.'

Mr Larch, already on his second glass, stretched his mouth in a rheumy approximation of a smile and said, '"The Lord God giveth and the Lord God taketh away."'

'Rum lot, you sky pilots,' said Sir Nimrod. 'The old Canon wouldn't have let the stiff out of his sight until it was safely packed in ice down at the morgue. But then the old Canon was a stickler for protocol.'

He glowered. In the old days before the final collapse of the Herring fortunes the living of Herring St George had been in the gift of the Herrings. Sir Nimrod, being High Church and conservative as well as Conservative, had always appointed Anglo-Catholics who spoke the Queen's English. Larch was a break with the tradition. He had been foisted on them by the progressive bishop of the diocese and Sir Nimrod regarded him as a closet Methodist. He had introduced a regular Family Mass, guitar music and a perfectly disgusting ritual called 'making the sign of peace with your neighbour'. This, Sir Nimrod, fuming in the family pew (a feudal vestige he still resolutely refused to relinquish), would have nothing to do with. He had not kissed another human being since Lady Hillary had passed on twenty years and more ago.

Parson and Squire, Bognor thought to himself. Or, in a manner of speaking, Squire Mark One (Sir Nimrod) and Squire Mark Two (Perry Contractor). Even now all English villages were supposed to have one of each, although in practice the parson was called something like a team ministry and was a handful of curates based on the nearest town and cruising round the surrounding villages when it suited them. Even Larch, he had learned from Peregrine, was nominally responsible for the smaller villages of Herring St Andrew and Herring All Saints, but All Saints was effectively delegated to the district nurse who doubled up as a deaconess and St Andrew was practically derelict. What passed for the St Andrew's congregation worshipped at St George except for twice a month when Larch took his guitar over for a People's Choral Evensong.

Bognor was a city person who had lived nearly all his adult life in London. He had all the townee's wariness about the country, suspecting that rural prettiness was merely a cover for incest, bestiality and possibly even witchcraft. Most of what he knew about village life was gleaned from reading the newspapers and a certain sort of novel.

'If this were fiction,' he muttered to his wife as they both helped themselves to another sausage roll from the hamper (Mrs Gotobed, the Contractors' cook had excelled herself) 'then we'd have the local doctor here as well, wouldn't we?'

'Him or the local bobby,' she agreed. 'I imagine we're about to get a visitation from Samantha's scrumptious policeman. Or do you think he's something she dreamed up?'

'Who knows?' asked Bognor more or less rhetorically. He really meant 'Who cares?' but was nervous of being overheard by his host or hostess. 'Frankly,' he went on, 'I'm beginning to wish I'd stayed in bed. These people all seem a bit peculiar.'

'Country air,' said Monica knowingly. 'Turns the head and ruins the complexion. Country folk always have addled brain cells and terminal skin cancer.'

'I'd forgotten how exhausting life was in the country.' Bognor sighed.

'It's not your surroundings that exhaust you, it's your time of life.'

There was some truth in this. Bognor would not see forty again. Come to that he felt he was unlikely to see fifty. In the days when the Clout first started a man of over forty was considered pretty antique, accorded much veneration and respect and not expected to live much longer. Bognor felt that he had been born into the wrong century. He felt like mediaeval man – course spent, sands of time run out – but was always being told that this was ridiculous. His contemporaries jogged, worked out with weights and ate nothing but nuts and sunflower seeds. Many of them persuaded themselves that they were in their prime of life. Worse still, many of them convinced very sexy women of half their age that they were in their prime of life. Bognor knew that, in his early forties, he had the body of a not very well preserved man in his late sixties. He just wished he lived at a time when this was regarded as normal. He did not particularly regret feeling so old; but he did object to being told he was peculiar. Never mind, the intellect was as sharp as ever.

There was a Tannoy system at the Clout; not a very sophisticated one, it crackled and whined through loud speakers placed on the corner of the mead tent and another by the St John's Ambulance post. The voice behind it belonged to Damian Macpherson, only son of 'Doc' and Mrs Macpherson. Damian was the village teddy boy. Although he was over thirty he seemed to be permanently unemployed and hung around in drainpipes, winklepickers and an old tail coat outside the pub. When anyone feminine passed by he would leer horribly and make various suggestions varying from a drink to a quick How's Your Father behind the cricket pavilion. But there was no malice in the man and no one had objected to his being appointed to the loud-speaker system. It was accepted that he would stick to the script and say nothing unless authorised by a member of the committee.

So far he had recited admirably, even injecting a note of sombre unflappability into the rather anodyne announcement about the body in the wood. Now, once more, he spoke:

'Would Mr Simon Bognor of East Sheen please report to Doctor Macpherson in the refreshment tent. Mr Simon Bognor to the refreshment tent.'

Bognor swore. 'I don't believe it,' he said. 'That can only mean one thing.'

Monica nodded, grim-faced. 'Parkinson,' she said.

''Fraid so.'

Just as she said it, Peregrine Contractor emerged from behind his Roller clutching a cordless telephone.

'Simon, old shoe,' he said, 'Dandiprat's on the blower. Your boss has been on in a state of excitement. Says he's been phoning everyone in sight. Wants you to check in p.d.q.'

Dandiprat was the Contractors' butler – very short, very obsequious and extremely sinister. He always gave Bognor the impression that he was in the possession of everyone's guilty secret.

'Unless I'm much mistaken he's been on to Damian Macpherson as well.' He sighed. 'Can I ring from the Rolls?'

'You'll reverse the charges?'

'Naturally.' Bognor knew perfectly well that a large part of Perry's success was due to an obsessive though selective parsimony. At the same time as he dispensed magnums of champagne he grudged you the price of a phone call. Entirely in character.

The phone was a push button cordless. Bognor, sitting in the back of the Rolls, punched 100 for the operator and waited. Not a lot of point, he reflected glumly, in a marvel of modern science like this car phone without visible means of support, when communications were fouled up by some incompetent human in the telephone exchange. When the operator did come on the line she sounded frumpish and surly, peeved at being disturbed. Bognor snapped at her and she snapped back, taking an age to put the call through and doing it gracelessly. 'I have a Mr Bognor calling from a Rolls Royce in Herring St George. Will you accept the charge?' he heard her say and was depressed to hear Parkinson saying, 'Yes, yes,' just as testily. He did dislike low spirits, particularly when they reflected his own. He liked other people to cheer him up. What was the point in people who simply depressed you?

Like Parkinson. Bognor's relationship with his boss was long standing and long suffering. There were those outsiders who regarded his marriage with incredulity, but this was unfair; despite a robust reluctance to be hen-pecked and a permanently wandering eye he was fond of old Monica. He was not fond of old Parkinson. Not a bit. And yet he had suffered under him for so long that life without him was unthinkable.

'Bognor?' That staccato almost derisive enquiry. He had endured it for so many years that now he accepted it and would have been uncomfortable if his superior began a telephone conversation in any other way.

'Speaking,' he said, just as tartly. It was not a one-sided affair. He gave as good as he got. Well, almost. At least he answered back. And if he did not answer back he was never servile. He had a good line in lip chewing, dumb insolence, an entirely justifiable attitude in view of Parkinson's permanent truculence and condescension. The trouble was that Parkinson while undeniably good at his job was in every other respect a comparatively low form of life. Bognor, although professionally miscast, was in every other way a person of the utmost distinction. It was a difficult situation to live with, though not uncommon. Bognor's experience of life was that it was not the cream which floated to the top but the scum. He and Parkinson were a case in point.

'I do apologise for disturbing your little holiday,' said Parkinson. As both of them knew full well, he did not mean what he said. Just the opposite. He liked nothing better than disrupting his subordinate's leisure time.

'That's perfectly all right,' said Bognor. This was also a lie.

'Not for the first time, Bognor, you seem to be bringing trouble where'er you go. You've conjured up a corpse from Customs and Excise.'

'You're remarkably well informed,' said Bognor drily. 'They only found him an hour or so ago.'

'The CID man in charge of the case is extremely quick on the draw,' said Parkinson, managing to imply that this was not quite the case with Bognor. 'Rather a ball of fire in fact. On checking him out I've discovered he's first rate. Absolutely first rate.' The inference was again quite plain.

'He's not called Guy, by any chance?' enquired Bognor, glumly apprehensive about a whizz kid who was also, on Mrs Contractor's evidence, what suggestible women nowadays referred to as a 'hunk'.

'Not by you, Bognor. As far as you're concerned he is Detective Chief Inspector the Earl of Rotherhithe.'

For once Bognor was able to trump his superior. 'In that case, sir,' he said, 'he's Guy. I was up at Oxford with him when he was plain Lord Wapping. He was a judo blue. Took my sister out a couple of times. Not my favourite person in all the world and neither as good looking nor as clever as other people seem to think. No real bottom.'

Now that Bognor was no longer on holiday but on official business, watching over the interests of the Board of Trade and liaising with Guy Rotherhithe, he judged it proper to move his HQ from the manor to the village pub. The Pickled Herring, for years a dozy unreformed public house dealing almost exclusively in mild, bitter, dandelion and burdock, had recently been purchased by an enterprising pair of gay entrepreneurs, Felix Entwistle and Norman

Bone. They were restaurateurs, Felix working front of house, Norman in the kitchen. Norman was an enthusiastic devotee of Nouvelle Cuisine, specialising in *magret de canard* and raspberry vinegar with almost everything. Last year the Good Food Guide had mortified them by removing their prized mortar and pestle though they still had the bottle for their wine list. The cellar was Felix's province.

The two men had refurbished the entire place with the exception of the public bar which in deference to local opinion, as articulated by Sir Nimrod, had been left untouched. It had flagstones, wooden pews and a dartboard. To the great irritation of Sir Nimrod an increasing number of the Herring's new upmarket clientèle had taken to barging into the public on the grounds that they found it 'real'. 'Real' was the new vogue word and could certainly not be applied to the rest of the pub which was filled with ferns and outsize teddy bears, chandeliers from Christopher Wray and even (in the gents) posters of Humphrey Bogart and Gary Cooper. Bognor rather liked it. It reminded him of Toronto.

He and Monica had checked into a double room called Myrtle. (Other bedrooms were Colombine, Hyacinth, Elderflower, Jasmine and Ragwort. Bognor rather liked the idea of Ragwort but it had no bathroom. Myrtle had a bathroom en suite. With a bidet.)

When Felix Entwistle had enquired how long Mr and Mrs Bognor would be staying, Bognor replied, grimly and with a touch of bravado, 'As long as it takes to solve the mystery.'

'What mystery would that be, sir?' asked Felix, to which Bognor made no reply but merely looked inscrutable.

'I think we're doing the right thing,' he said in the privacy of Myrtle. 'We can't very well stay with Perry and Sam if they're under suspicion of having anything to do with it.' He sat on the edge of the bed and stared moodily at an indifferent print of a Tom Keating Samuel Palmer.

'Who said anything about Perry and Sam being under suspicion?' Monica was snappish. She did not at all like the Pickled Herring and had been all for going home to the London suburbs. Bognor had seemed so miserable when she said this that she had melted and remained. She had married him for richer for poorer, for better or worse and she supposed she ought to stand by him, tiresome though it might be to be holed up indefinitely in the middle of nowhere.

'Guy,' said Bognor. 'Guy says that everyone must be regarded as under suspicion until proved otherwise. He says this is a very suspicious village. He says he's had his eye on it for some time, mainly on account of the swami's outfit. Not that I'm inclined to believe what Guy says. He really is a bit of an ass.'

Bognor had had a brief but relatively inconsequential encounter with the chief inspector earlier in the morning shortly after his conversation with Parkinson. The two men had agreed to meet for a drink around six in the lounge bar to discuss tactics. Bognor was not much looking forward to it.

'I think Guy's right for once,' said Monica irritatingly. She had always rather fancied Guy in the old days and the hint of grey he now had at the temples rather enhanced his appeal. 'Personally speaking it gives me the creeps. There's something spooky about the place. I know you think Phoney Fred is just a joke but I think he's positively dangerous. Some of his so-called acolytes can't be more than twelve. All junked out of their minds by the look of it.'

The swami, otherwise known to villagers as Phoney Fred, had taken over Herring Hall five years ago. Ever since, rumours of drugs, sex, drink and all round zombie-ism had abounded.

Like so many modern mystics the swami was exceedingly rich, exceedingly hairy, and exceedingly attractive to nubile young women. All of this annoyed Bognor who was none of these. He could have grown a beard if he had wanted but the wealth and sex appeal were depressingly elusive. The swami drove around in a series of vintage motor cars, mainly Bugattis. He was almost always accompanied by a wife. He had an enormous number of wives, known formally as the Brides of the Chosen. The wives wore white. The swami, naturally, wore saffron and sandles as well as a leather strap about his neck from which there hung a leather pouch. This contained small pieces of blank coloured paper which he was accustomed to present to people with a wide smile and a mumbled blessing. The bits of paper were supposed to be very lucky. One purporting to be autographed by him had fetched several thousand guineas at auction.

The villagers of Herring St George tolerated the swami and his followers with a long suffering scepticism. This was reasonable enough for generally speaking they kept themselves to themselves and paid the rates. They did not patronise the Pickled Herring nor did they attend church. When they first bought the hall from a property developer who was unable to obtain planning permission for an Olde English Theme Parke it was widely thought that they would try to take over the community rather like that other, not wholly dissimilar, sect in Oregon. But as the weeks passed the villagers realised that the swami was not going to stand for the parish council or try to convert them to whatever it was that he believed in. The swami's people (the Blessed Followers of the Chosen Light, to give them their English title – there was another in Sanskrit) had a regular weekly order from the village shop and Sir Nimrod never conquered his disbelief about the amount of grapefruit juice they drank. When Naomi Herring called to sell poppies in aid of the Earl Haig fund just before Remembrance Day the swami personally wrote a cheque for a hundred pounds and kissed her on both cheeks. She said later that he smelt terribly of joss stick.

'I think he's pretty harmless,' said Bognor. He had a curious optimism even about proven villains. Had he been around in the thirties he would have been inclined to think Hitler and Mussolini 'pretty harmless'.

'He's no more a swami than you are,' said Monica. 'Underneath all that face fungus and filth he's as white as us.'

'I didn't say he was real,' said Bognor. 'Obviously he's a fraud. I bet he's a Balliol man. At least I bet he claims he was at Balliol.' He paused. 'Fraudulent, sticky fingered and over-sexed; but there are plenty of people like that. It doesn't make them killers.'

'I don't understand why it couldn't have been an accident,' said Monica. 'Chap gets very drunk, goes to sleep in Gallows Wood and is riddled with arrows by the villagers before he wakes up. QED if you ask me.'

'According to Parkinson, Wilmslow hardly touched alcohol,' said Bognor.

Monica smiled. 'All the more reason for him to go to sleep under the old oak tree. He obviously didn't have a head for it.'

'But he wouldn't have drunk it in the first place.'

'But he did, didn't he?'

Bognor pursed his lips and nodded a touch glumly, 'They reckon so. We won't know until the tests come through.'

Monica sighed. 'All right,' she said. 'You and Guy think he was murdered because he was drunk and being drunk wasn't in character. That's a bit flimsy. Anything else?'

Bognor scratched the back of his head where the hair was thinnest. 'I'll know more when the files arrive. Parkinson's having them sent down by courier. We don't really know what exactly he was investigating but Parkinson implied that it was a lot more than simple VAT irregularities. If we can find out exactly what or who he was on to, then we'll have a motive and a suspect.'

'Does Guy have any ideas?'

'He's going through all Wilmslow's things. Presumably he'll turn up some sort of notebook. Some of those sort of people use portable computers. There may be a disk.' He walked over to the window and looked out on to the green, so perfect an example of British Tourist Authority

England that it could have been run up by Disney. It didn't go with corpses, not at first glance, but Bognor had always been suspicious about countryside. In his view cities were much safer.

'I still think it was almost certainly an accident,' said Monica. 'The trouble with people in your line of work is that you're so melodramatic. You always subscribe to conspiracy theories. You always find niggers in woodpiles. You always make life complicated when it's actually incredibly simple. It's so boring of you.'

Bognor shrugged. 'That may be so in everyday life,' he said, 'but in my line of work, as you perfectly well know, it's always wise to look on the black side and believe the worst of everyone and everything. I believe in original sin and universal guilt, and...' he broke off for a second '...if I'm not much mistaken I think I see a ministry motorcyclist heading this way with a whole load of bumf from Customs and Excise.' The thunder of Japanese horsepower cut through the somnolence of late afternoon, reached a crescendo and then suddenly stopped very cleanly, leaving a silence more silent than before.

Bognor called down to the despatch rider, a burly man in late middle age.

'Do you have a package for me – Simon Bognor, Board of Trade?'

The messenger looked suspiciously at Bognor, hesitated and then decided to make no reply. Instead he rummaged in one of his panniers and produced a large brown padded envelope. Without looking up again he walked towards the front door of the Pickled Herring with an air of considerable gravitas.

'Oh, God, I hate motorcyclists,' said Bognor, furiously.

'He may not be for you,' said Monica. 'He may be bringing truffles hot foot from Perigord or the first of the season's grouse as felled by Viscount Whitelaw.'

'Don't be ridiculous.' Bognor was not amused. 'It's not even August. Of course it's for me. It's one of the office

29

messengers. I've seen him countless times in Whitehall. He knows perfectly well who I am. Stupid oaf!'

He stomped out, slamming the door. Monica stared after him bleakly, then flopped full length on the bed and began to read a rude novel by Wendy Perriam. She supposed she loved her husband but he could be an awful bore. His time of life, she supposed; she personally believed men went through just as bad an emotional crisis in their early forties as any woman at any stage in her life. Bognor was like a passed over major or a perpetual curate. He had no serious prospects of advancement and yet he had to soldier on until he took early retirement and a pension. Quite a grim prospect, she could see that; but there was no need to be quite so beastly so often. She would have to talk it over with him. Woman to man.

It was a quarter of an hour before he returned pink and bothery but definitely triumphant. He held the very large brown envelope which he had already opened, messily, so that the kapok stuffing was spilling out all over the very expensive, dense, macaroon-coloured carpet.

'God, what a palaver!' he said. 'Identification in triplicate; four signatures. I'm surprised he didn't want a birth certificate or a reference from the vicar.'

'Personally,' said Monica, 'I'm rather pleased. It's nice to have some secure security for a change.'

'Don't be pompous,' said Bognor. 'He knew perfectly well who I was, he was just being difficult.'

'That, if I may say so,' said Monica, saying so, 'is the sort of attitude which led to Burgess and Maclean and that man Prime at GCHQ.'

'Now you really are being pompous,' he said, falling into a fussy chintz armchair and removing a wad of papers from the envelope. 'There is absolutely no similarity whatever between me and Guy Burgess or Geoffrey Prime.'

'I do so hate it when you deliberately misunderstand me,' said Monica. She glowered briefly and returned to her Wendy Perriam.

Bognor too began to read. There was an awful lot of stuff, much of it quite irrelevant and footling. Like so many of his colleagues, Wilmslow had been a tree not a wood man. Or, more accurately, a twig man. His papers were full of triumphal discoveries of restaurant bills where the fifteen per cent of VAT had been added before rather than after the service charge; of phone bills where businesses had been trying to claim back VAT on what were clearly personal private calls; of zero ratings being claimed on invalid imports; of muddles between input and output. Wilmslow would not have had a chance, reckoned Bognor, of seeing Birnham Wood for the stage props. Never. His eyes never strayed from the small print taking care of the pennies while the pounds took care of themselves. Bognor, who had good grounds for believing that some large and clever companies were perpetrating genuine frauds on a massive scale was outraged. It confirmed everything he had always believed.

The Herring St George papers were not the only ones there and for a while, as he riffled through the pile, Bognor even wondered if they had been omitted altogether. That too would have been bloody typical.

He found them in the end, however. Like the earlier stuff they were a mixture of typing and Wilmslow's characteristically tiny, punctilious handwriting. A nitpicker's hand. Not many people in the village were registered for VAT. It required an annual turnover in excess of eighteen thousand pounds and although the character of the place had changed drastically in recent years the new affluence was not, on the whole, self-employed. Moreover the weekenders, of whom there were several, were registered in their town homes and would be visited by Wilmslow or a colleague in London.

The first few names were exactly as Bognor had expected: The Society of the Blessed Followers of the Chosen Light, PLC (SBFCL), Herring Hall. He knew perfectly well that the swami's lot had considerable international holdings, not least in North Sea Oil.

The Village Stores, Herring St George. This was a very different story but even though Sir Nimrod's profit margins were undoubtedly modest, VAT was a turnover tax, not an income tax.

The Pickled Herring, Herring St George. Larger profits here for Felix and Norman, though not yet vast.

Fashions Sous-tous PLC, The Manor House, Herring St George. Bognor knew that although Peregrine Contractor employed no fashion staff – either production or design – at the Manor it was nonetheless the base for all his operations thanks to the wonders of modern computer technology.

There were just two other VAT registered people, one of whom he should have thought of. Doc Macpherson was a high enough earner, even under the National Health scheme, to qualify. But the final entry was quite unexpected: Emerald Carlsbad, author and self-employed therapist.

'Emerald Carlsbad!' he said out loud, 'Who she?'

On the bed Monica, immersed sulkily in her novel, did not reply.

'Emerald Carlsbad,' repeated Bognor, 'The New Maltings, Herring St George. I wonder where that is. Means nothing. Funny name and funny occupation. Not much need for therapy in Herring St George even in this day and age.'

He turned the page and found photostats of old VAT returns from the various registered parties. No great surprises. The swami and Peregrine Contractor were turning over hundreds of thousands of pounds every three month tax period. Doc Macpherson was doing nicely thank you and must have had a sizeable private practice to supplement his income. Poor Sir Nimrod was all input and very little output. Desperate attempts to get the Excise to reimburse seemed to have failed on every occasion, usually as far as Bognor could make out because the wretched squire emeritus had failed to fill in the form properly. Indeed to add insult to injury he had been fined quite heavily for tick-ing the box marked 'exempt outputs' when he had meant to tick 'bad debt relief'. It was obviously too much for him.

'Village stores seem to be in a pretty parlous state,' he said.

'So would you be if you sold nothing but gumboots and Grape-Nuts,' said Monica.

'What do you mean?' Bognor had not been to the stores. 'It's a village post office and general shop. That sort of place sells everything: gobstoppers, safety pins, cat food, Bird's Custard, cod liver oil.' Bognor's eyes glazed. He was remembering his childhood.

'*Au contraire*,' said Monica, 'gumboots and Grape-Nuts. Nothing else at all. I went in there for Alka Seltzer after that first evening at the Contractors. No Alka Seltzer. No Fernet Branca. No Paracetamol. No Prairie Oysters – not even an egg, let alone Worcester Sauce. No Aspirin. Nothing but gumboots and Grape-Nuts. Oh, and some very old bacon with curling rind and just a hint of mildew and verdigris.' She shrugged and subsided on to the counterpane.

'Are you sure?'

'Of course I'm sure. The gumboots are suspended on lengths of string, though they probably call it "twine" round here, and the Grape-Nuts are in crates. He's proba-bly got the left overs from the Everest Expedition.'

'Horrible things to have for breakfast,' said Bognor with feeling. 'So gritty. They stick in your teeth. But surely he has sugar and milk to go with them?'

'*Rien du tout*.' Monica pouted. 'It's a disaster. They can't be making a bean. In fact if you ask me it's amazing he can afford to eat or drink. Nobody shops there any more, they all drive in to Whelk and go to the mall.'

Whelk, the county town, had one of the most modern shopping precincts in the country. You could buy every-thing from a whole sheep butchered specially for your freezer to enormous economy packs of loo paper which people stored in their nuclear fallout shelters. And there was Muzak.

'I should have thought Naomi would have managed to get the place ticking over,' said Bognor. 'She seemed moderately normal. The old boy is more or less barking I grant you but surely she could run a village shop?'

Monica did not reply, and Bognor continued to study Wilmslow's papers frowning at the small print, the fiddly handwriting and, above all, the endless figures. He had always disliked maths and been sceptical about finance. No doubt there were secrets hidden away in all these forms and bills and receipts but Bognor was not optimistic about teasing them out. It would take a man like Wilmslow to do that – the sort of person who could spot a falsely calculated percentage at a glance and knew by instinct that 'Box 1 + Box 2 + Box 3 should equal Box 4' and that 'Box 4 – Box 7 should equal Box 8 (if tax is due)'. Bognor was not like that, not at all; and so it was not long before he put the file down promising, half-heartedly, to attack it again after dinner, and walked to the window, humming a tenor aria from one of the Mozart operas whose name he had temporarily forgotten.

'It looks like straightforward VAT stuff to me,' he said, gazing down on to the green.

'No such thing,' said Monica.

'As what?'

'Straightforward VAT stuff. It's always convoluted. Never what it seems. That's why it was invented in the first place. It's an excuse for spying on us. VAT inspectors can come into your house without so much as a by-your-leave, beat the place up, steal all your papers and there's absolutely nothing anyone can do about it. They can get away with murder.'

'Not Wilmslow,' said Bognor sourly. 'Wilmslow was one VAT inspector who didn't get away with anything.'

'Which still doesn't mean he was murdered,' said Monica.

Bognor frowned. 'I have a funny feeling,' he said, 'that we're not going to have a lot of trouble coming up with motives. In fact I'll bet you dinner at Tante Claire that there are at least three people in Herring St George who would have liked to see Wilmslow dead.'

'You have to do better than that,' said Monica, 'I don't like VAT men and I'd happily see most of them dead; but that doesn't mean I'd actually murder one. The motive has to be really strong. Not just disgruntlement. Has to be passionate loathing or pathological fear.'

'Passionate loathing or pathological fear,' agreed Bognor, a touch grudgingly.

'Then you're on,' said his wife.

THREE

Guy Rotherhithe drank Perrier water. 'He would, wouldn't he?' thought Bognor as he ordered a large gin and tonic from Ben, the barman in the small dark bar which used to be the Snug and which was now called Popinjay's. Ben mixed a drink called a Popinjay which was a gin sling made with strawberry liqueur topped with a miniature fruit salad and one of those small bamboo parasols. Monica had tried one and pronounced it 'interesting'.

Drinking Perrier all the time was one of the reasons, Bognor supposed, that Guy Rotherhithe looked like Guy Rotherhithe, just as drinking gin and other alcoholic drinks quite a lot of the time was the reason Simon Bognor looked like Simon Bognor. Now that they were wallowing through their forties Bognor and his friends and contemporaries were beginning to reflect their life styles. There was no escaping the fact that Bognor did look a mite seedy just as Guy Rotherhithe looked extremely chipper. If you played squash and jogged and drank no alcohol you looked like Guy; if you were largely sedentary and ate and drank what you felt like you looked like Simon. Fact of life. Simon would rather like to look like Guy but he told himself that his life style was the more enjoyable. In any event it was too late now to change.

'I'm not at all sure I like the look of things,' said Guy, when they had found a quiet table in a quiet corner. It was very dark in the bar and the subdued lighting which just highlighted the brass buttons on Guy's blazer and the silvery pennants on his yacht club tie made him look even more unbearably handsome than he did in daylight. 'This is a very unorthodox little village: swamis and knicker manufacturers and God knows what else. There's a rumour that some writer chappie's moving in to the old watermill. He made a fortune out of a book about a parrot; writes about TV for one of the Sunday papers.'

'That's Kingsley Amis' boy Martin. He writes Litero-nasties; HPH.'

'HPH?' Guy sipped Perrier water; as he leaned forward the silver at his temples flickered suddenly, then merged into dark again.

'Hard porn for highbrows,' said Bognor. 'It's the in-thing. The parrot was stuffed. It used to be that the only writers who lived in villages had initials and pipes: J.B.Priestley and H.E.Bates. Now they're all called Julian.'

'You said Martin,' said Guy.

'Did I?' Bognor was unabashed. 'It's all the same thing. I suppose I'm getting old. Anyway if he hasn't moved in yet he can't have murdered the VAT man. Writers don't kill people except in print.'

'The Carlsbad woman's supposed to be some sort of writer,' said Guy. 'But we're having a job finding out what exactly it is that she writes. Only one title under her own name and that's hardly likely to account for her declared income.'

'What is it?'

'*Freudian Traumdeutung in the Cook Islands*. Two Volumes. Published in 1947 and 1950.'

Bognor looked as blank as he felt. Then he said: 'Freudian, eh?'

'Yes.' One of Guy's eyebrows could just be seen to rise quarter of an inch in the gloom. 'Why?'

'She's down in Wilmslow's files as "therapist",' said Bognor. 'I wasn't sure what that means. In view of *Freudian Traumdeutung in the Cook Islands* I take it we can assume she's some sort of psycho-therapist?'

'Plenty of scope for that sort of thing in Herring St George,' said Guy poking at his lemon with a toothpick.

'You think so?'

'Sure so.' Guy sighed. 'There are those nutters up at the hall. Phoney Fred's lot. Doc Macpherson's boy Damian. Old Sir Nimrod's got a screw loose or two. And...' He paused and then said, darkly, 'There are others.'

'Such as?'

'Well...' Guy suddenly seemed to be experiencing tremendous difficulties with his lemon, 'No names, no pack drill.'

'You mean the Contractors?'

'I didn't say that.' Bognor knew perfectly well that was who he meant. Even when he was Lord Wapping Guy Rotherhithe had not been a creature of subtlety. When he put his foot in it, which was often, he had fearful difficulties getting it out again.

'Do you know something about the Contractors that I don't?' he asked.

Guy abandoned the lemon and crossed his legs.

'I don't know what you know about the Contractors,' he said uneasily.

'Listen Guy,' Bognor leaned towards the immaculate blazer and his paunch brushed the table top. 'If we're going to co-operate on this case then we're going to have to co-operate. You level with me and I'll level with you. It'll be hopeless otherwise. If there's something you know about the Contractors then I think you should tell me.'

Guy swallowed. 'There's nothing I can prove in a court of law,' he said. 'Nothing criminal.'

'What then?'

'Well, you know, parties and things.'

'Parties and things?' Bognor was incredulous. 'Since when were parties and things an offence?' he said. 'Of course they have parties. They're party people. Boxes at Ascot; boxes at Glyndebourne; knees-ups in Annabel's. They're in the *Tatler* and *Harpers* every month. It's all part of the image; good for business. He's going to have his own polo team next summer. Trying to get Prince Charles to play. Of course they have parties and things.'

'I don't mean that sort of party,' said Guy, 'I mean...well you know... Sex...and drugs.'

Bognor still affected astonishment.

'I never thought of you as a prude, Guy,' he said, smiling. 'But I suppose it's all these years as a country bumpkin. Nowadays lots of parties are full of sex and drugs. If you're part of the fast set that's what you expect. It's normal.'

'That the sort of party you and Monica go to?'

Some of Bognor's gin went down the wrong way and he had a brief splutter of coughing.

'We're...' he tried when he had regained his powers of coherent speech 'not really like that. Never been ones for gadding about and we're alcohol people as you know. Rather behind the times. But if you're into gadding about, then it's sex and drugs all the time.'

Even in the gloom Guy did not look very convinced. 'From what I hear,' he said, very seriously, 'this isn't just horseplay: not just canoodling and cannabis. It's hard drugs and serious sex. Orgies. And if it were to get out there could be a scandal. If my sources are correct then it's that fatal combination of call girls and cabinet ministers. Judges too; but no bishops.' He smiled grimly. 'They're not the best company to keep, Simon,' he said.

'Well,' Bognor back-pedalled a little, 'in my line of work it's as well to keep informed. We've had our eye on the Contractors, we at the Board of Trade. It's not just for pleasure that Monica and I have cultivated them you know. But I must say I'm surprised. They sail a bit close to the wind now and then but I'd be surprised if they were running orgies. They've certainly never asked us to one.'

Guy said nothing, just gazed at Bognor and looked knowing. One eyebrow raised a little and the corner of his mouth twitched. Bognor was finding him extremely trying.

'The point is,' said Bognor, 'that standards in town are not like standards in the country. What seems perfectly acceptable up there may seem over the top down here. What seems normal in Herring St George would often seem antediluvian in town. I dare say people round here dress for dinner and wear three-piece tweed suits for church.'

'That's all changing,' said Guy morosely. 'I mean look at this.' He waved a hand around the bar. 'It's not so long ago that this was a regular old-fashioned pub with skittles and mild and bitter. Now it's a poncy wine bar run by a couple of pretentious Nancy boys. There's a chapter of Hell's Angels at Nether Pillock; the Mayor of Whelk was done for interfering with boy scouts at the annual camp last Whitsun; and you've seen for yourself what's happened to Herring St George. You might as well live in Golders Green.'

'Nothing wrong with Golders Green,' said Bognor. 'My mother-in-law lives in Golders Green.'

'You know what I mean,' said the chief inspector. 'Everywhere you look it's spivs and wide boys, tarts and con men. If this is what the Prime Minister means by a return to Victorian values she can keep it. I'd rather live in New Zealand.'

'Oh, I don't know,' said Bognor, weakly.

'Well I do,' said Guy. 'As far as I'm concerned the bottom's fallen out of this country. Moral fibre gone to the dogs. Anything goes. Everyone wants something for nothing and devil take the hindmost. It's bloody awful, frankly. And there's nowhere that's more symptomatic of the decline in civilised standards and values than the English village. Used to be the salt of the earth, English villagers. And now look what's happened, they've either emigrated or gone to live in housing estates in Whelk. And all we've got here is a lot of weekenders in sheepskin jackets and crocodile brothel creepers. Makes you weep.'

'You're not old enough to talk like that,' said Bognor. 'You're not allowed to be that reactionary until you're eighty. Not unless you're a brigadier or belong to the National Front.'

'It's not reactionary, just reality,' he said. 'And this latest business is a symptom.'

Bognor was not keen on this right-wing popular sociology.

'Well,' he said, 'that's all very well but what we have to decide is whether a crime has been committed, and if so by whom.'

'Perfectly simple,' said Guy, 'to let the coroner bring in an accidental death verdict, even if it's hedged around with a few doubts and ambiguities. It looks pretty accidental on the face of it.'

'Except that he didn't drink.'

'Did your people say that?' Guy did not sound surprised.

'Yes,' said Bognor.

'Confirmed by the people here at the Pickled Herring.' The policeman swallowed the last of his Perrier and signalled for another round. 'Never seen with more than a half of bitter or maybe a single glass of the house plonk with a meal. He could make either last for an eternity.'

'But he was drunk when they found him?'

'Stank of alcohol. Haven't had the autopsy reports yet but either way I presume they'll show an uncharacteristically large intake of alcohol.'

'Either way?' Their second round of drinks materialised and Bognor signed for them, wondering as he did whether there was going to be another boring row with boring Parkinson about boring expenses.

'Either he drank it voluntarily or it was poured down him by what we professionals usually call a person or persons as yet unknown.'

'A third party,' said Bognor.

'Just so. It seems unlikely he drank whatever he drank of his own accord. He had dinner here on his own; then went into the lounge and drank coffee while he watched the news.'

'Then went to bed,' ventured Bognor.

'The bed hadn't been slept in,' said Guy. 'He had a standing order for morning tea at seven. When the maid went in the sheets were turned down and the complimentary After Eight mint was still on the pillow where it had been put the night before.'

'So where did he go after the news?'

Guy shrugged. 'No idea,' he said. 'We found a diary in the room and he'd got nothing down for that evening. He was seeing your friends the Contractors the following morning and Emerald Carlsbad the day after that. In other words he logged his appointments very conscientiously. So if there was nothing down for that evening he can't have had anything planned.'

'So something cropped up at the last moment. Or someone.' Bognor frowned. It was looking more and more like crime. 'There's no way he could have wandered off into the night clutching a bottle of Scotch?'

Guy Rotherhithe shook his head. 'Had it been you...' he said.

Bognor chose to ignore this gibe, though it did not go unrecorded.

'What we're saying,' he said, 'is that we have no idea what the hell Brian Wilmslow was doing between nine twenty-five and this morning when he was killed at the Clout.'

'If he *was* killed at the Clout,' said the chief inspector darkly.

'You're implying he was murdered during the night and dumped in Gallows Wood.'

'Yes.'

'Now why,' said Bognor, 'would anyone do a thing like that?'

'Why which?' asked Guy with an unexpected sharpness. '"Why murder?" is one question; "why dump?" is quite another.'

'If he *had* been murdered already, then he was presumably dumped so that we would think he was killed by the arrows. And if he *was* killed by the arrows there's no telling whose arrow it was. Who knows who pulled the string.

It's like that Agatha Christie where they take turns stabbing the man on the train.'

'*The Orient Express*,' said Guy.

'Albert Finney in a hairnet,' said Bognor, who was not that keen on Dame Agatha's work, mainly because the solutions were always so neat and unlike his experience of real life. 'The point is that if he was murdered by one of the archers we've no way of knowing which one.'

'My point precisely,' said Guy. 'No better way of spreading the blame than to arrange for your victim to be skewered by the entire population.'

'Just suppose,' said Bognor after a pause while they digested their hypotheses, 'just suppose that someone sandbagged him or doped him or alcoholled him into some sense of false security; and just suppose that that someone left him in Gallows Wood knowing full well that he was in the line of fire from the massed archers of the Popinjay Clout. Now would that person be guilty of murder? Always supposing that Wilmslow was still alive when he was abandoned in Gallows Wood. What do you suppose?'

'You sound like my old chief constable, Lejeune of the Yard,' said Guy. 'Let us suppose this...let us suppose that. He was the ultimate pedant. Always had to go through every letter of the alphabet to get from A to B.'

'You haven't answered me,' said Bognor relentlessly.

'My answer,' Guy sighed, 'is that whether or not such a person is guilty, and if so of what, is no concern of mine. That's what judges are for. All I know is that if we have reasonable grounds to suppose that X or Y abducted Wilmslow and left him in Gallows Wood on the morning of the Clout then it is our duty to arrest X or Y. What happens after that is none of our affair.'

'Now *you* sound like Chief Constable Lejeune.' Bognor was, as always, irritated by this nitpickish worrying of the bones of the case. He wanted to get on with it. And yet his experience was that without this attention to detail, to unturned stones and ludicrous hypotheses, you never got anywhere at all. You could create the illusion of progress but it was quite false. Detection was a tortoise and hare affair. It was his main complaint about it. 'Put it another way,' he said carefully, 'if he really did have too much to drink and blundered into the wood to sleep it off, then there's no real case to answer. Death by misadventure. Person or persons unknown.'

'That's not what happened,' said Guy.

'But you don't know that.'

Guy grinned. 'I've never been more certain of anything.'

Bognor frowned. 'That's intuition. You aren't allowed intuition in our game, you know that. It's inadmissible. "How did you know that Professor Plum did it in the conservatory with the poker?" "Intuition, my lord." It wouldn't wash. Case dismissed. We need a rational progression of facts leading inexorably to a logical conclusion.'

'Quite,' said Guy. 'Nevertheless intuition can play a part in directing you to asking the questions which elucidate the facts. In any event I intend proceeding on the basis that there was foul play. I think Wilmslow was interfered with. Whether he was alive or dead when he was abandoned in the wood is neither here nor there. The court can play around with that. Our job is to find out who put him there – dead *or* alive.'

'I see,' said Bognor.

'So the first thing I shall do,' continued Guy decisively, 'is to have a chat to all the people on Wilmslow's list and get them to account for their movements between the end of the nine o'clock news and breakfast.'

'What about motive?'

'Sod motive!' said Guy, who had obviously been transformed by the Perrier. 'Let's find out who did it. Once we've done that we'll get the reason soon enough.'

Bognor wondered whether he should order another gin and decided against. Not because he didn't want one but because he didn't want the police thinking he was some sort of lush.

44

'In that case,' he said, 'I think I'll concentrate on motive. We'll be approaching it from two different ends of the stick.'

'One of the ends is bound to be the wrong one,' said Guy. He laughed with the rather gratified air of a man who has been surprised by a joke he had never intended.

'Not necessarily,' said Bognor, managing to imply a depth of hidden meaning which he hoped he was not going to be called upon to reveal. He was happier with the shady ambiguities and semi-conscious neuroses implicit in dealing with people's reasons for wanting to kill other people. Guy's self-appointed role of investigator of times and places of alibis and whereabouts struck him as mundane and unintellectual. The difference, to his way of thinking, between philosophy and algebra. But then he was only a modest arts graduate. Also he was well aware that in the upper reaches of academe there were plenty of dons who would tell him that algebra and philosophy were one and the same. Perhaps that was what he meant about there being two right ends of this particular stick.

He was saved from these not entirely relevant musings by the entrance of Monica, Mrs Bognor. She did not enter Popinjay's in the prescribed Chandler manner, carrying a smoking gun, but she might almost have done for she was clearly the bearer of dramatic tidings. Her air of disarray and incompletely applied lipstick suggested, even to men like Bognor and Guy Rotherhithe, that she had been interrupted in mid toilette.

'I was hoping I'd find you two boys in here,' she said. 'Can I have a quick drink? Sir Nimrod's in the bedroom and I'm not going back without one of you.'

'Good grief!' said Bognor. 'You don't mean...'

'Oh don't be so ridiculous,' said Monica, eyes flashing through the artificial gloaming. 'And get me a large Scotch. I hate this dump. Give me the North End Road any day.'

Bognor thought of saying something crisp but went to the bar instead where he ordered his wife's whisky and

45

surreptitiously procured another gin for himself. The Inspector was still only halfway through his Perrier.

When he returned to their table he found Guy grinning in a way that he knew Monica would resent. Condescending. It implied that Monica was a piece of fluff to be humoured but, in serious matters, ignored. This was a dangerous misapprehension.

'It sounds as if you've got your man,' said Guy. 'Squire Herring's come to confess.'

'That is not what I said,' Monica said frigidly as she took a gulp of her drink. 'Thank you darling,' she added in a tone which was not so much intended to thank her husband as to put the policeman in his place.

'What then?' Bognor smiled at Guy in a half-hearted attempt to warn him to take Monica a touch more seriously.

'He wants to talk to you,' said Monica. 'He said it's very important. It's about Brian Wilmslow and he's extremely agitated.'

'Why didn't he come down?'

'He said he wanted to talk to you in private.'

'Was it wise leaving him alone in your room?' Guy's manner was half mocking, half plodding. Like a Gilbert and Sullivan policeman; and not in a professional production either.

'Oh, don't be so bloody ridiculous.' Monica's voice rasped down her nostrils like Maggie Smith's at moments like this.

'I'm not being ridiculous.' Guy was stung. 'He may be the murderer for all you know. And if he's in any way involved he'll be having a good look through those Board of Trade papers by now.'

'Those Board of Trade papers,' said Monica slowly, emphasising each word, 'are locked safely in Simon's briefcase. Besides which Sir Nimrod is safely locked in our room as well. It seemed a sensible precaution.' She took a second swig of Scotch and stared at the handsome policeman, challenging him to say something else stupid.

'Sorry,' he said, then glanced self-importantly at his watch. Bognor half expected him to say that he had a train to catch, or, worse, that he had work to do. Instead he said quite flatly, 'I have an appointment. No doubt you'll tell me all about Sir Nimrod in the morning.' And with his irritatingly even-toothed smile and an ingratiating genuflection in Monica's direction he was off and away.

'Conceited ass,' said Monica. 'I can't stand those sort of superficial good looks.'

Bognor knew this was not a good moment to gloat.

'We'd better go and unlock the squire,' he said.

He had his back to them when they entered the room and seemed for a moment unaware of any intrusion. Only when Bognor coughed did he turn from the window with a surprised shake of the head, like a man emerging from a dream which, it immediately transpired, was just what he was doing.

'We came here from Caen,' he said, blinking.

Mr and Mrs Bognor looked blank.

'William d'herring. Knight. Namesake of the Conqueror. Came from Caen.' The incongruous tuft of ginger hair waggled curiously as he spoke. 'We're nearly all in the vault. You realise I'm the twenty-third baronet and when I'm gone the title passes to my cousin Keith in Canterbury.'

'That's not so far,' said Bognor, grasping at straws.

'About twenty-four hours as the crow flies,' said the old man. 'Six weeks by P and O.'

'Canterbury, New Zealand, you idiot,' hissed Monica, spitting in his right ear. Bognor nodded. Keith was clearly a Kiwi.

Sir Nimrod was obviously not finished. He was nowhere near the point. Bognor was about to ask him to come to it a little more rapidly but stopped himself, realising that this was probably a case of 'softly, softly'.

'The whole of English history's in the Herring family tree,' continued the squire. 'Forget all that clever stuff they teach you at Oxford and the London School of bloody Economics. You don't need a lot of damned Marxists banging on with their half-baked theorising – it's all here in Herring St George.' He rubbed a rheumy eye and repeated, 'All here in Herring St George and when I'm gone it's finished.'

'Perhaps your cousin Keith will come home and settle.'

Monica meant to be soothing but Sir Nimrod only glowered. 'Whole damned country's gone to the dogs or New Zealand,' he said and sat down heavily in a high-backed porter's chair which Felix had picked up in a junk shop in Whelk. It was covered in nutmeg brown velvet. 'Fact of life. God knows we might as well have let Hitler and his chums in. It couldn't have been worse than it is and at least the trains would run on time.' He paused and looked thoughtful. 'Was it Hitler who made the trains run on time or Mussolini? There hasn't even been a station in Herring St George since that fat oaf Beeching axed it. And they've taken the dining car off the eight-thirty from Whelk to town. Would you believe the station's just been bought by some writer chap for over a hundred thousand? Writes tea commercials. Something to do with monkeys.'

Bognor felt it was time to impose a little order on these ramblings.

'Monica said you had something to tell me,' he said, not unkindly but with officer-class authority. 'About the death this morning.'

'You wouldn't have such a thing as a drink would you?' The old man rummaged in his pocket and produced a packet of cheap thin Woodbine cigarettes. The Bognors always had a bottle of Scotch in their hotel room. Bognor poured a thimble into a tooth mug and added water. When this was done and the Woodbine was alight Sir Nimrod said: 'Look at the Clout. The Clout was going even before we got here. Hundreds of years. Happy family occasion. Private affair. Now it's day trippers and cameras and even journalists.' He pronounced the last word 'jawnalists' and he pronounced it with a dreadful contempt.

'Oh, not really a journalist,' said Bognor, trying to maintain a light tone, 'a gentleman from *The Times*.'

'Gentleman from *The Times*!' Sir Nimrod spat the words out. 'It's owned by some friend of cousin Keith. There hasn't been a gentleman on *The Times* since that rat Northcliffe took it over.'

Bognor swallowed and decided to restrict himself to business.

'What exactly was it you wanted to tell me?' he asked, quite briskly this time.

This time there was a very long pause. Bognor realised that much of the squire's meandering so far, while heartfelt, was really a device to put off the difficult moment when he had to say what he had come to say. It was obviously a message he had qualms about delivering.

'You're some sort of intelligence wallah?' he hazarded at last.

'In a manner of speaking,' admitted Bognor. 'I work for the Board of Trade in Special Investigations.'

'Ah.' Sir Nimrod chewed this revelation for a while but obviously found it difficult to digest. He tried another tack.

'You're investigating this morning's business. The body and all that?'

'Up to a point,' said Bognor unhelpfully.

'Up to what point?' asked Sir Nimrod, reasonably enough.

'My husband is assisting the police with their enquiries,' said Monica. 'The chief inspector is in charge but my husband has a sort of watching brief on behalf of the government.'

'Much rather not talk to the police. Delicate matter.'

Neither Simon nor Monica knew quite what to make of this and after a while the squire continued. 'The fact is,' he said, 'that chap they found in the wood this morning was a bit of a skeleton in my cupboard if you follow my drift.'

'I see,' said Bognor, now hopelessly adrift.

'You do promise that this won't go beyond these four walls?' He looked searchingly at Bognor who started to reply cautiously but was over-ruled by his wife who said, bossily, 'Anything you say will be treated in the utmost confidence.'

She gave her husband one of her celebrated 'for heaven's sake shut up and be sensible' glances.

'The fact of the matter,' said Sir Nimrod at last, 'is that this creature Wilmslow who was done in during the Clout is the son of our old butler, Wilmslow.'

There was a long pause while the Bognors digested this unlikely revelation and wondered where it was going to lead.

'Very difficult to explain this,' he continued, 'but they were a bad lot those Wilmslows. Father came to us through an advertisement in the *Lady* and I never was sure about his references. My wife was alive then, God bless her, and she said I was imagining things.'

He lit another cigarette. 'You see the fact is,' he said, 'that Naomi's not her mother's daughter.'

'I don't follow,' said Bognor.

'She's Edith's girl.'

'Edith?'

'Mrs Macpherson. I...well, to put it bluntly, Edith and I were walking out together...'

'You mean you and Edith Macpherson had an affair and Naomi was the result?' Monica did not mean to be gratuitously rough but she felt it was time to cut some cackle.

'I suppose so,' said Sir Nimrod wretchedly.

'I don't understand,' said Bognor. 'Why didn't you all get divorced?'

'Edith wanted to go back to Macpherson,' said Sir Nimrod staring at the floor. 'But he wouldn't have her back with the child.'

'So you took her on and pretended she was your wife's child. That must have been rather difficult.'

'Very difficult time,' agreed Sir Nimrod still avoiding any eye contact. 'Muriel never got over it.'

Bognor remembered Peregrine and Samantha telling him about Lady Herring's faintly mysterious demise in the moat.

'But how...I mean surely people noticed...' Monica, for once, was groping, 'I mean surely people would have realised that Mrs Macpherson was pregnant and that Lady Herring was not. It's not easy to conceal these things. I don't mean to seem indelicate but someone must have noticed. Especially in a tight little English village like this one.'

'The ladies both went away for several months,' he said, so softly that he was barely audible. 'I seem to recollect that we said something about going abroad. You must remember this was more than forty years ago. There was a war on. Strange things happen in war. I make no excuses but they were unusual times. Very unusual.'

'And how exactly does the butler, Wilmslow, come into all this?' Bognor had a pretty good idea, of course. But he wanted to hear it from the horse's mouth.

Sir Nimrod swallowed hard. 'Wilmslow found out,' he said. 'He was a rat. I'd have had to sell up anyway. Damned socialists saw to that with their damn fool taxes. And I was never much of a farmer. But we could have hung on a lot longer if it hadn't been for Wilmslow.'

'Blackmail?' asked Bognor, dropping his voice in sympathy with the man in the confessional.

Sir Nimrod nodded.

'I'm sorry to be brutal,' said Bognor. 'But I want to be absolutely sure I've got this right. You're telling me that Naomi is the illegitimate daughter of you and Edith Macpherson; that your butler, Wilmslow, discovered this and blackmailed you over it.'

'Yes,' said Sir Nimrod miserably.

'And then what?'

'He bled us white, and when there was nothing more to

take he took off. To Spain. He sent a card at Christmas.'

'And did the blackmail continue?'

'Off and on. He wasn't stupid. He could see I was cleaned out. I sent him one or two... Tokens really. I think he only asked so that I wouldn't forget he had a hold over me. He was that sort of person. Utter shit.'

'Had you heard from him recently?'

'Christmas cards stopped about ten years ago. I assumed he'd dropped dead or found fatter fish to fry. And then the son turned up.'

'Just like that?'

'What do you mean, "just like that"?' Sir Nimrod looked suspicious.

'No warnings. No letters. No telephone calls.'

'Just came into the shop three days ago, said he was Mr Wilmslow from Customs and Excise and he wanted to inspect the books.'

'And did he?'

The village postmaster looked sheepish. 'The books ...well, the books weren't altogether in order. I told him so and he said he'd call back after the weekend.'

'He didn't try to blackmail you?' asked Monica.

'He's not stupid. No point in trying to bleed a corpse.'

'Did he say anything about his father? About old times?' Bognor scratched his scalp. What the old man said was true enough. He was virtually destitute. There was scarcely any visible means of support, let alone any sign of a blackmail-able fortune.

'Not a word.'

'And you didn't say anything? You didn't ask him if his father was still alive?'

Sir Nimrod shook his head. 'I wouldn't give him the satisfaction,' he said grimly.

'You are sure it was him?' asked Monica. 'It must have been a long time since you last saw him?'

'Over twenty years, but it was him all right. There's a Wilmslow look you can't mistake. Spitting image of his father, he was. A nasty chip off an extremely unpleasant block.' Sir Nimrod drained his glass. 'I couldn't have the other half?' he enquired plaintively. 'No fun baring the soul like this.'

'I can see that,' said Bognor, while his wife replenished the glass, 'which makes me ask why you're doing it?'

'Thought it best if you heard it from me,' said the old man. He rubbed at his ginger whiskers. 'It wouldn't have looked too good coming from someone else.'

'You're right,' said Bognor. 'On the face of it you had an extremely plausible motive for wishing Mr Wilmslow dead.'

'No bones about it, old boy.' The squire was either very relieved at having got the confession off his chest or the whisky was relaxing him. 'I'm glad he's gone and, given the chance, I'd have done him in myself.'

'But with respect,' said Monica, 'he seems to have behaved just as any ordinary VAT inspector would have done. Do you think he remembered who you were? I mean how old was he when he left the village?'

'Late teens,' said Sir Nimrod. 'He was a teddy boy. Drainpipe trousers and winklepickers. Ludicrous figure. He remembered all right. You could see it in his eyes.'

'So,' persisted Monica, 'if he didn't come here to blackmail you, then what did he come here for?'

Sir Nimrod shook his head. 'Can't imagine. To gloat perhaps. And the little sewer obviously *was* a VAT inspector, too.'

'Well you're quite right in one respect,' said Bognor. 'If someone else had told me this then I'm afraid I'd have marked you down as a suspect straight away. No mistaking the fact it's one of the strongest motives a chap could have.'

'That's what I felt.' He seemed almost jaunty compared to his earlier despair.

'Well thank you for coming.' Bognor smiled gratefully at the scruffy figure with his stained Eton tie and creased tweed jacket, leather-patched at the elbows. Life had dealt harshly with this last of the Herrings. 'Just for form's sake,' he added pleasantly, 'we might as well establish your alibi. It's by no means certain that foul play was involved; but if there was foul play it seems likely to have taken place between about nine-thirty at night and breakfast next day. Where were you then?'

Sir Nimrod pursed his lips: 'There was a Clout committee meeting at the Macphersons,' he said. 'That was over by about half past eight. I walked back, had supper and then stayed up with Naomi till two a.m. wrestling with the wretched accounts.'

'And up pretty early in the morning to get ready for the Clout.'

'Always up at five-thirty,' he said, smiling wistfully. 'Always used to have an early reveille for milking. Incurable habit I'm afraid. I'd break it if I could.'

He drained the remains of his second drink.

'Glad I've got that off my chest,' he said. 'Can't tell you how much it's been bothering me. You promise it won't go any further? It would break my heart if Naomi were to find out.'

'Naomi doesn't know?'

'Good grief, no.' He stood up and slapped invisible crumbs from the knees of his sadly decayed corduroy trousers. 'Perish the thought.'

The Bognors also stood.

'It was good of you to come,' said Bognor. 'I'm most grateful.'

'It's a weight off my mind I don't mind telling you.'

'You haven't discussed it with the Macphersons?' Monica smiled sweetly but for a moment Sir Nimrod seemed to hesitate almost as if, for the first time, there had been a deviation from the script. 'We don't talk about it,' he said. 'Water under the bridge if you know what I mean. Water under the bridge.'

'So the Macphersons never knew that Wilmslow was

blackmailing you?' If Sir Nimrod Herring had known Monica Bognor a little better he would have been very wary of that smile which was not very enthusiastically reflected in her deep brown, restlessly perceptive eyes.

'Absolutely not!' he said. 'My own secret. A cross I suffered in silence. I make no excuses. My behaviour was unforgivable even allowing for there being a war on. But it's been a hard row to hoe. A very hard row indeed.'

He made for the door. 'Naomi's stewing rabbit,' he said, 'rabbit with forcemeat balls. She's a stickler for punctuality, so I'd better totter back p.d.q. Awfully good of you to listen so patiently. You know where to find me if you need me.' He paused with his hand on the door and looked Bognor up and down appraisingly, 'You quite sure you're no relation of old Theo Bognor? You've got the same nose, there's no question about it. That's a Bognor nose all right.'

'It's possible,' said Bognor. 'It's not a very usual name. But not as far as I know.'

'Ah well!' He turned the handle, 'Must rush. Toodle pip!'

FOUR

The dining room of the Pickled Herring was as determinedly serious as Popinjay's bar was not. It was so plainly discreet that you screamed for some sign of excess – gilt, for instance, on chandeliers, or one of those colossal Franglais menus with fulsome descriptions of every dish's provenance. Instead it was all sensible modern chairs, school of Conran; spotlights shining on to pine and plain white napery and plain, heavy glasses. There were four starters, three main courses, four desserts and a small number of dishes of the day recited by Felix. Felix was so unobtrusively, beautifully dressed that you scarcely realised he was there: very very light grey flannels, an American-style blazer, a creamy silk shirt and a very very pale plain beige tie with matching pocket handkerchief. Smoking was not allowed and you felt that it would be grossest sacrilege to ask for a salt cellar or any spirits other than (perhaps) a very rare single malt whisky to drink after the frangipani sorbet with kiwi fruit.

'I don't like the look of this much,' said Bognor. 'I'm famished.'

'It'll do us both good,' said his wife without conviction.

'I do not wish to be done good,' said Bognor, 'I do not want *magret de canard* with ginger and raspberry vinegar nor ceviche of swordfish marinated in dill nor calves' liver in a sauce of elderflower wine and wild Wiltshire truffles.'

'No,' said Monica. 'Do you think we should slip out and find a fish and chippy or a take out tandoori?'

'Too late,' said Bognor, 'Felix is coming to take our order.'

Felix recommended the dishes of the day in a tastefully discreet whisper and they both, reluctantly, ordered breast of guinea fowl in a choux pastry. Bognor chose a decent claret from the gratifyingly decent wine list. Only when this had been accomplished did he finally say, 'Well what did you think of Sir Nimrod's confession?'

Monica nibbled a minute *bouchée* of Boursin-flavoured brioche.

'It's a jolly odd story,' she said eventually.

'He's quite an odd cove.'

'That's incontestable,' she agreed.

'Not to say barmy.'

'That wouldn't be pushing it too far.'

'I don't see Naomi as a child of passion.' Bognor took the last of the cheesy appetisers which melted away in his mouth as tantalisingly as candyfloss.

'Well be reasonable, darling, she is forty, if she's a day. I mean frankly you don't look as if you were conceived in an act of fine careless rapture yourself.'

'I say,' Bognor was put out, 'steady on.'

'I'm not being personal. No one does, much, once they've passed the six-month mark. I agree it's difficult to imagine Sir Nimrod having a bit of a fling, but we're talking about forty odd years ago when he was younger than us.'

'*Cave*,' said Bognor, 'Felix is coming back. With bad news by the look of it. He's wringing his hands like a frustrated washerwoman.'

It was rather bad news. If it had been a different sort of place and Felix a different sort of person he would have said simply, 'Guinea fowl's off.' Instead of this he said, 'I am most terribly sorry, sir, madam, but there appears to have been the teensiest bit of a crossed wire in the commissariat and it seems that we're down to our very last guinea fowl.' He fixed Bognor with a fraudulently obsequious smile in the style of Uriah Heep and said, 'We do have some very good fillet steak which Norman could flash under the grill for you.'

If there was one thing Bognor was exceptionally partial to it was fillet steak, just the well done side of *sanglant*. 'Well,' he said, 'in the circumstances I'm prepared to be a bit of a martyr. Madam will take the last guinea fowl and I'll make do with the boring old steak. Never mind. Can't be helped.'

As Felix went on his way Monica skewered her spouse with a wounding glance that would have deeply unsettled someone less used to them than Bognor of the Board of Trade. If looks could kill Monica Bognor's would have been the facial equivalent of the black mamba or that peculiarly lethal spider which lives in Australia. Over the years however Simon had developed an impressive immunity. Nevertheless the hostility of this one was so marked that even he flinched.

'*Qu'est ce que c'est?*' he enquired dutifully. 'You look as if you've swallowed a prune lightly sautéed in raspberry vinegar and garnished with kiwi fruit.'

'Pig!' said Monica. 'Selfish pig!'

'What do you mean, "pig"?' Bognor was affronted and genuinely surprised.

'Don't you "what do you mean, pig" me, Simon Bognor,' said Monica her voice rising ominously. 'First of all you force me to stay down here in this hell hole and then you have the effrontery to order steak when I'm stuck with a mingy bit of raw pigeon in a poncy piece of puff pastry.'

'But you ordered pigeon. And it wasn't pigeon it was guinea fowl.'

'I don't care, I don't want it. And you know perfectly well I don't want it. I want to go home. No one ever offered me steak. It's the most disgusting form of sex discrimination. Typical. Men get steaks while women have to make do with itty bitty little bits of bird wrapped up in fussy flakes.'

Bognor decided that a tactical withdrawal was in order.

'O.K.,' he said, 'have the steak.'

'No, no,' Monica was getting worryingly near the edge. 'You have the steak. I'll make do with the guinea fowl. You're a man. You need the steak. Why don't you have it raw with a handful of red chillis and a flagon of foaming ale?'

'This is silly,' said Bognor. 'If you want the steak have the bloody steak. If you don't want it then have the guinea fowl. I really don't mind. I just want you to be happy.'

Monica glowered.

'All right,' she said, eventually, 'I will.'

'Good.' Bognor smiled. 'And I'll have the guinea fowl.'

'Yes,' said Monica.

Bognor knew from years of experience that the correct procedure now was to leave bad alone. If you pursued the matter Monica would flare up, remaining in full volcanic eruption for quite astonishingly long periods. If ignored, however, she subsided, quite fast. She was inclined to smoulder for a while but provided one said as little as possible there were no more explosions.

After what seemed like a very long time Monica said: 'I suppose it could have been a sort of double bluff.'

For a moment he thought she was still talking about the steak. Just in time he realised she was talking about Sir Nimrod Herring and checked what might have proved an incendiary response.

'Go on,' he said cautiously.

'Well,' she said, 'if Wilmslow was trying to blackmail him again and if he did murder him then coming to you in a burst of honesty would be likely to throw you off the scent. As it has.'

'But he's drawn attention to it. If he hadn't said anything no one else would have said anything about it either. I'd never have known.'

'Not necessarily.' Monica smiled as Felix bought the claret, a bourgeois growth she couldn't pronounce, and they paused while Bognor sniffed and gurgled plausibly enough to satisfy everyone's amour-propre. When Felix retired

Monica said, 'If you and the police were conducting a murder investigation, there's no telling what might come out in the wash. Including the extra-marital affairs of the nineteen forties.'

Bognor said he supposed that was possible though if it had been his skeleton in his cupboard he would have kept quiet about it and hoped no one would find out.

'Typical man!' said Monica, but if she was hoping to elicit an immoderate response she was having no luck. Her husband preferred a quiet life if he could get it – which was not often. Presently their first course arrived. It appeared to be ducks' livers in a savoury custard with a garnish of carved radishes. Two mouthfuls each.

'Still,' said Bognor, 'even if there's something fishy about Sir Nimrod's story I can't regard him as a suspect. He's too old and batty.'

'An accomplice?'

'Conceivably.' Bognor sipped the wine. 'But I don't see whose at the moment. I'm inclined to take him at face value. The blackmailing butler's son turns up unexpectedly and drops dead probably murdered by person or persons unknown. Old Herring knows he's got a motive and that if anyone finds out then fingers are liable to be pointed. So he comes along and owns up.'

'Thus putting himself in the clear.' Monica sounded suspicious.

'Correct,' agreed Bognor. 'But wanting to establish your innocence isn't an acknowledgement of guilt. We're not *that* cynical, surely?'

'I suppose not.' Monica did not seem very sure but her uncertainty was curtailed by the advent of their main course borne in by Felix who seemed to be doing everything tonight. Lucky it was a quiet evening.

'Guinea fowl for madam,' he said, beaming suavely at Monica.

'Er, no,' said Monica. 'Steak for madam. Guinea fowl for sir. We had a change of plan.'

Felix seemed oddly obstinate. He put the pastry case on the mat in front of Monica and said, 'If you'll allow me, madam, I think that the guinea fowl has just that little subtlety and refinement of taste which madam will enjoy.'

He could not have said anything less tactful. Monica was no conventional feminist. She had a considerable antipathy to most card-carrying feminists, frequently on less than rational grounds. She had never liked Germaine Greer, for instance, since reading somewhere that she never shaved her armpits. The *Guardian*'s women's page infuriated her because one of its leading contributors had been at school with her and edged her out of the lacrosse team. But Monica did have one thing in common with her more strident sisters. She did not like to be patronised.

'I said,' said Monica, icily, 'that my husband is having the guinea fowl. And I am having the steak.'

Felix appealed to his fellow man.

'The steak is just as you asked,' he said, 'a little more cooked than rare with just a hint of red wine and local herbs.'

Bognor did not remember any mention being made of red wine or local herbs. But that was beside the point.

'My wife and I,' he said, 'changed our minds. She very sweetly decided to let me have the guinea fowl in pastry as it's something of a speciality of the house. And she feels very much like a steak. You know how sometimes one...well one does feel like a steak.'

Felix still did not relinquish his hold on the steak which looked and smelt extremely appetising.

'Madam,' he said, 'the *magret de canard* is exceptional. A great speciality of the house and particularly fine tonight.'

Monica stared at him. 'Listen,' she said, 'I don't for one instant see why you have chosen to make such an issue but I would be obliged – we would both be obliged – if you would give me my steak and him his guinea fowl before they get cold. I simply do not see that who eats which is the slightest concern of yours. If either of them is less than edible we shall send them back.'

Say what you like about a convent education, it can make a woman exceedingly fierce in her middle years. Felix blanched like any mere vegetable exposed to steam; deposited the plates as instructed; and retired to the kitchen. Seconds later however he re-emerged accompanied by Norman Bone in full cheffly fig, toque at a rakish angle as if put on in great haste.

'I'm afraid there has been some mistake,' he said.

Monica glared up at him, the first morsel of meat transfixed on her fork and halfway from plate to mouth. 'No mistake,' she said. 'No mistake at all.'

Norman's hand reached out towards the plate. 'I, that is, I just happened to look at the rest of the steak and I have a terrible feeling it may be just that little bit over the top. I couldn't possibly run the risk of your going down with a gippy tummy. If it was salmonella the health people would close us down.'

Bognor was somewhat alarmed by this but Monica sat her ground. 'If you don't mind,' she said, 'I will be the judge of that. If it tastes off I shall send it back. I've already told your colleague I'll do that. And if I go down with food poisoning that's my affair. I shan't prosecute. And my husband is with the Board of Trade. He will guarantee that there's no trouble from the authorities. Is that all right?' And she put the steak into her mouth, chewed briefly, swallowed and drank an eighth of a glass of wine. Then she smiled glacially at the joint patrons of the Pickled Herring. 'Perfectly delicious,' she said, 'just as I like it. Thank you both so very much!'

The two men glanced at each other, shrugged, and returned whence they had come, muttering but vanquished.

'Actually,' said Bognor, a little morosely, 'this guinea fowl isn't at all bad. A bit anaemic but that's to be expected. It's very tender.'

They ate on in silence.

'A bit heavy on the tarragon,' said Bognor, 'but the pastry's light as anything.'

'Knock me down with a pastry,' said Monica, with her mouth full.

'I beg your pardon,' he said.

'I thought you were going to say light as a feather.'

'I stopped myself just in time,' said Bognor, who had been taught that the use of clichés even – no especially – in conversation, was the sign of a lazy mind. 'How *is* the steak? I mean really.'

'The meat's delicious,' said Monica, chewing thought-fully, 'but I'm not a hundred per cent certain of the sauce. It's on the bitter side.'

'Some local herb, no doubt,' said Bognor, 'ragwort or dandelion root.'

'Could be,' agreed Monica. 'It's not unpleasant, just bitter. Perhaps that's why they made such a fuss. Perhaps it's a special masculine herb unsuitable for ladies.'

'An aphrodisiac you mean? The rural English equiva-lent of rhinoceros horn.'

'I didn't say that.'

'It would explain that extraordinary performance, though,' said Bognor. 'Very rum. Never seen anything like it. Not even when old Escoffier Savarin Smith was in charge at the Dour Dragoon.'

'Poor old Scoff,' said Monica. Scoff had been murdered. Bognor had solved the crime.

'How did you get on with Guy before I arrived?' asked Monica. 'He's an awful stuffed shirt. A real tailor's dummy.'

'I thought you fancied him.' Bognor regretted this remark as soon as it was uttered.

'Me? Guy? You must be joking.'

'He didn't have anything very interesting to say,' said Bognor. 'He's going to plod about the place asking ploddy questions about people's whereabouts at crucial times.'

'Meanwhile you zoom around conducting snappy

interrogations about id, ego, Oedipus complex and whether or not the deceased was having an affair with someone.'

'No need to be sarcastic. You know quite well that that kind of thing is my forte.' Bognor had always considered himself a fine judge of character, a shrewd analyst of personal behaviour, and an outstanding critic of the broad sweep of history and current affairs. He had little time for dates which, like addresses, telephone numbers and other 'facts' were best kept in books where they could always be looked up. Any fool could do that. He liked to keep his mind uncluttered so that it could deal with nothing but essentials.

'I wasn't being sarcastic,' said Monica. 'Really.'

Bognor smiled. Things appeared to be improving and there were no disagreements over their desserts – jellied fruit salad in a pastry basket for her, a chocolate and almond sorbet with crystallised mint leaves for him. Then coffee from a brass and glass *cafetière* left on the table with tiny squares of healthfood fudge.

'What plans for the morning?' she asked, stifling a yawn.

'I thought I'd start with the mysterious Emerald Carlsbad. She intrigues me. We know less about her than almost anyone in this set-up and her VAT papers are peculiar. Too much money to be explained by therapy and psychiatry. Unless she has some extraordinary practice in Harley Street or wherever high-class shrinks hang out these days.' He also yawned. 'Quite a day,' he said, 'I think I'm going to pack it in and try for an early start. What do you imagine they give you for breakfast – poached kiwi fruit?'

FIVE

Bognor was renowned as a very heavy sleeper. He often had trouble getting to sleep, especially as he had a phobia about sleeping pills, but once there, snoring heavily (Monica assured him) he was almost impossible to wake. When woken he very quickly had all his wits about him, as he was quick to remind her. If there was a burglar in the house Simon would have chopped him with a poker before he could say knife once he was awake; but Monica claimed that on occasion he had slept for twenty-three and a half minutes after she had stuck a bar of sandalwood soap in his mouth and secured his nose with a large paperclip. 'Why didn't you wake me?' he would protest when she complained of a night disturbed by his gutturally whistling nostrils. Then she would attack him with pillows or hairbrushes or whatever lay close at hand.

When, therefore, he suddenly sat up in bed and saw from the bedside alarm that it was twenty past two he realised that something was badly wrong or very noisy indeed. Turning to his left he saw that his wife was not with him. Then he heard a wretched moaning and gagging sound from the bathroom. Leaping from the bed he hurried in and found Monica slumped over the lavatory, heaving and retching.

It was on the tip of his tongue to ask if she was all right but he realised the fatuity of the question just as he realised that she was almost beyond speech. Quickly he knelt down beside her. Her forehead was streaming with sweat and her face had virtually no colour left.

Monica was never ill. It was always him. Suddenly he felt

very lost.

'I'll call a doctor,' he said.

She moaned.

'Don't move. I'll be right back.'

He hurried back into the bedroom, grabbed at the phone, then wondered what on earth to do. He would hardly get room service in a country pub, however pretentious, at this hour of the morning. He could only get an outside line by going through the hotel's miniature switchboard and that would hardly be working at 2 a.m. either. The one thing he could not do was nothing. Despairing he dialled 'O' and to his amazement heard a click from the other end of the line before there was even a ring.

'Yes. Can I help?' It was Felix's voice, sounding very awake and quite alarmed.

'It's Simon Bognor in, er, Myrtle. My wife...I think you must have been right about the steak. She's very sick. I think we need a doctor. Or perhaps an ambulance. I don't want to be melodramatic but she's very bad.' From the bathroom a further spasm of moaning and retching could be heard. 'She seems to have a fever too.'

Bognor was not entirely clear what was happening at the other end of the line but he could hear muffled voices. Presumably Felix was talking to his partner, Norman. They presumably shared a bed since they appeared to share everything else.

'Mr Bognor, are you still there?'

Bognor said 'yes', impatiently. He was anxious to get back to his wife even if he could do nothing more useful than hold her hand and wipe her brow and say 'there, there'. He suddenly realised that if anything were to happen to her he'd be quite upset. 'Please God, don't let her die,' he said to himself and then heard Felix say, 'Don't try to move her whatever you do. Just let her stay exactly where she is until Doctor Macpherson gets to you. He should be there in a jiffy.'

And, amazingly, even as these words were uttered, he

heard heavy hurrying footsteps, two pairs, followed by a knocking on the door. He cast aside the telephone, feverishly adjusted his ageing Viyella pyjamas to make himself as presentable as possible, and rushed over to the door. It took him a moment to release the chain and unlock it (you couldn't be too careful even in Herring St George, especially after what had happened to Wilmslow) and fling it open. There, breathing heavily in the corridor, was Norman Bone in a shantung bathrobe, black, embroidered with crimson poppies. Beside him was a thin, etiolated figure in striped trousers and a black jacket. He carried a worn black grip with the initials 'E.St. G. MacP.' embossed on one side. Bognor recognised it as a doctor's bag of pre or immediately post war vintage, not from personal experience but from watching black and white films of that era on late-night television. Such bags were invariably carried by Miles Malleson and other character actors. They were often cinematic code for imminent birth.

'Doctor!' said Bognor, slipping unconsciously into vintage celluloid argot. 'Thank heavens you've come!'

For a giddy moment he thought Macpherson was going to say 'I just happened to be passing' but instead he just pushed past rather roughly, opening his bag as he did. He passed through into the bathroom and closed the door behind him, leaving Bognor and Norman Bone, standing there looking at each other sheepishly.

'That was quick!' said Bognor, a shade fatuously.

'Pure luck,' said Bone. 'He just happened...that is he was here already. I woke half an hour ago with this perfectly fearful migraine. Doctor Macpherson says I must call him out whenever I get one in case it turns out to be some form of haemorrhage. He says I'm rhesus something or other. Not negative or positive. More exotic than that. Anyway I'm a very high risk so he always comes straight out at once in case it's a real emergency and I have to be rushed into Whelk General. He's a tower of strength, Doc Macpherson, and so imaginative. He gave me acupuncture for my sinuses and the most amazing homeopathic remedy for piles. I do hope your wife's all right. I blame myself I really do. I should never have let her eat the steak. Well I shouldn't have let either of you eat the steak. I said to Felix, the second I smelt the rest of it, I should never have done it. Never. Listen I brought a bottle of the Hine VSOP with me.' He removed a bottle from the pocket of his dressing gown and passed it to his guest. 'Have a taste of that. I'm sure she'll be all right. He's wonderful in emergencies.'

Bognor took a swig. 'You'd better come in,' he said. From the bathroom there was a sound of moaning coupled with the unmistakable drone of bedside manner of an old school; a reassuring litany of placebo and panacea designed to shut the patient up and make him or her submit unquestioningly to whatever indignities were being inflicted. Seconds later the bedroom door was opened by the good doctor, now in braces and shirtsleeves, and with his thick silvery mane dishevelled though in an attractively bouffant style which might have been pre-arranged.

'Bognor, old chap, I wonder if you'd be good enough to give me a hand getting your wife back into bed. She's a bit of a handful if you'll pardon the expression.'

Bognor handed the Hine back to Norman and stepped through into the bathroom. Monica was no longer moaning. Her eyes were shut and she was breathing deeply.

'You take her left and I'll take the right. You'll find she's a dead weight.'

Bognor had never manhandled an unconscious wife before; it was invariably the other way about. He was surprised to find quite how heavy she was. Or perhaps it was a decline in his own muscle power. Together however they half dragged half carried her to the four poster and heaved her up. Bognor tucked her in, while Macpherson produced a stethoscope and checked her breathing. Then he felt her pulse, frowning at an old fob watch as he did.

'Is she going to be all right?' he asked.

'Yes, yes,' said the doctor, allowing Monica's hand to fall

to her side – a little roughly in her husband's opinion.

'Is she asleep?' Bognor accepted the proffered brandy from Norman and passed it on to Macpherson. The doctor drank deeply. And Bognor realised that he had caught a distinct whiff of booze on his breath the second he came in the door.

'Asleep?' Macpherson put his head on one side, and regarded the patient with a quizzical smile. 'In a manner of speaking. You'd probably call it a trance. Hypnotic. It's surprising how quickly you can put someone under if you know how to do it, and, naturally, if they're a good subject. Your wife's a remarkably good subject, Mr Bognor. In fact I would guess she's blessed with considerable psycho-kinetic powers. Does she have premonitions ever?'

'Well.' Bognor frowned. 'Not in the sense that she'll tell you there's going to be an air crash or an earthquake the day before it happens. She's very prescient but I put that down to intelligence and a certain amount of intuition.'

The doctor eyed him sceptically. 'You would, would you?' he said, suddenly sounding unexpectedly Aberdonian. It had all been Home Counties up until now.

'Is she going to be all right?' Bognor asked again, ignoring the pointedness of the remark and not in any case seeing exactly what point Macpherson was attempting to make.

'She'll be right as rain in the morning,' he said. 'And she won't remember a thing about it. She'll be weak naturally so let her spend the morning in bed. Toast and tea for breakfast. No alcohol till after the sun's over the yard arm. Call me if you're at all concerned about anything.'

'What else did you give her?' Bognor was aware of sounding shrill. He felt he was not in control of events. 'You didn't just hypnotise her?' The brandy was back with Norman Bone. Bognor thought he caught a flicker of conspiratorial concern between the two men. It was the slightest suggestion, a mere hint of a hint. Given the stress of the moment he might well have imagined it. But he thought not.

'A wee jab,' said the doctor. 'A little cocktail. Nothing very strong. Homeopathic if you understand what that means. It doesn't always apply but in a case like this it's the best and surest remedy.'

'A case like what?'

This time Bognor was certain that a silent message passed between Bone and Macpherson.

'Let's just say that she would appear to have consumed something that did not agree with her. It's easily done. And if everything turns out well then the least said about it the better. Isn't that so, Mr Bone?'

'That's my view, Doctor.'

Macpherson beamed down at his hypnotised patient. She was breathing very deeply but quite regularly. The fever seemed to have diminished.

'Don't try to wake her before morning.' The doctor smiled at Bognor. An expression not entirely devoid of menace. Bognor looked into the eyes to see if they matched the expression of the lips. There were many people who claimed to be able to sniff out hypocrisy by studying men's eyes. Parkinson for one. Bognor, however, did not subscribe to the theory. If a con man was half good at his job he could get his eyes to participate in the con just as effectively as any other part of his body. The notion that a man's eyes were some sort of gateway into his soul was the purest gobbledygook. No better than mediaeval superstition. You might as well judge someone by the stripes on his tie. The doctor's eyes seemed, to Bognor, to be totally noncommittal. He could not conceivably say whether they were for him or against him. Only that they were disturbingly blood-shot. Fleetingly Bognor remembered that they were the eyes of a man who, forty years before, had been cuckolded by Squire Herring.

'I'll be going then,' said Macpherson. 'Absolutely no cause for alarm. Good night to you.'

And they saw themselves out, both smiling thinly, as they

left Bognor alone with his unconscious wife and some half formed but disturbed and disturbing thoughts. For the first time on this case he was alarmed and fearful because he had the strongest possible suspicion that what had happened was no accident.

He re-chained and locked the door, turned off the light and swung himself into bed alongside his heavy breathing wife.

It must have been the steak. He retraced the sequence of events. He and Monica had both ordered the guinea fowl which was one of the day's specials in an extremely under-crowded restaurant. The odds against their having genuinely run out were incalculably high. Felix had manoeuvred him into having the steak because the steak was the easiest dish to doctor. They had probably infiltrated some poison into the sauce. Inedible fungus perhaps. Monica had complained that the sauce was unnaturally bitter. That could explain it.

Lying in bed he experienced a sudden chill of fright and put out a hand to grasp his sleeping wife's. They had meant to kill him. It was the only explanation. That was why they had tried so hard to make him eat the poisoned fillet and why they had been so anxious not to let Monica eat it. Why they had almost panicked. And that story about Norman's migraine. Poppycock. They had alerted the doctor so that at the first sign of symptoms he could come beetling upstairs and administer an instant antidote. Which meant that Doc Macpherson was part of the conspiracy as well.

Why had they baulked at killing Monica? They had no qualms about killing him. Was it a panic measure by the two hoteliers – one which would have been reinforced by the doctor no matter who the victim? And if it was a panic measure what prompted the panic? They would have rea-lised that he was conferring with Chief Inspector the Earl of Rotherhithe. But that was no reason for murder.

They could well have known that Sir Nimrod had come to call even though he had gone straight to 'Myrtle'. They thought Sir Nimrod had blown the gaffe. But what gaffe? How could Felix and Norman possibly be concerned with the true parentage of Naomi Herring. Both, Bognor guessed, were no more than late thirties which made them younger than Naomi. It didn't make sense. Alongside him Monica breathed deeply in her hypnotic trance. But Bognor could not sleep. Try as he might he could not unravel the mysteries of the night nor ease the sudden realisation that this thatched and rose clad pocket of forever England was as personally threatening as any jungle – concrete or tropical.

He must have drowsed off because he never heard the maid with the morning tea and *The Times* and *Telegraph*, not even when Monica dragged herself out of bed and swore at him for having locked the door and put it on the chain. It was the drop of Earl Grey spilt (deliberately it has to be said) on his chest by his loving spouse which brought him round.

'Jesus Christ, what on earth did you do that for? I'll have to have a skin graft.' He felt fighting fit for a moment but the mood swiftly passed as he remembered what had happened during the night. 'Are you all right?' he added solicitously, reaching out to touch Monica's forehead. It felt very cool.

'Yes.' Monica had bagged *The Times* and was fishing in her handbag for the Portfolio card. They had never yet won at Dingo but as they frequently reminded each other there was a first time for everything.

'Not sick?'

'Not in the least.' Monica removed the pencil from the spine of her Liberal-SDP Alliance diary (a facetious present from Bognor) and started filling in the Portfolio entry. Quite a jolly joke playing bingo with share prices in the once-upon-a-time top people's newspaper.

'Doc Macpherson said you'd probably feel rather weak.'

'I always feel weak in the mornings. You ought to know

that by now.' She scribbled in some numbers, frowning as she did.

'We agreed you should spend the morning in bed.'

'I should love to spend the morning in bed,' she said, 'but not if you're going to be here pestering me. I'm afraid if that was rhinoceros horn in the sauce last night it had no effect whatever. I feel about as randy as a blancmange.'

'Don't you remember anything about last night?' asked Bognor.

'Only that I slept extraordinarily well.' She put down the newspaper and stared at him, plainly perplexed. 'It's a very comfortable bed.' She continued to stare. 'What did you say about Doctor Macpherson?'

'He said you'd feel weak.'

'What in God's name does Doctor Macpherson know about it?'

Bognor scratched his baldish patch. Then he said: 'Don't scream for a minute. I want to get through this without interruption. O.K.?'

Monica examined him sceptically for a moment. 'I promise not to scream until you've finished talking,' she said. 'After that I feel free to do as I please.'

Bognor nodded. 'O.K.,' he said. 'Now you remember the steak?'

'Don't say too much about the steak.' Monica sipped tea. 'Or I shall consider myself discharged from all promises.'

'The steak is crucial. You'll have to bear with me. I'll make it as quick as I can. Let us suppose, as Guy Rotherhithe's old boss Lejeune of the Yard would say, that Felix and Norman want to murder me.'

'Why?' asked Monica, not unreasonably.

'Shh,' said Bognor. 'We're playing this by Lejeune's law. When proceeding in a westerly direction from A to B always plod. A is our first supposition, viz that Felix and Norman want to kill me. The obvious way to do so is to slip something in the meal they're preparing for me. This, however, is difficult if either (a) I order something that is already prepared or (b) we order the same thing.'

Monica nodded patiently.

'The first part of their plan went flawlessly. In other words they succeeded in persuading me to have a steak. God knows what they put in it. It probably was a lethal fungus of some description. Or maybe they keep some paraquat derivative floating around. I don't know. Anyway, their plans go hopelessly askew when Felix comes back with the killer fillet and finds that you, that is to say we, have changed our minds.'

'Careful,' said Monica, 'I shall scream if you're rude.'

'Whereupon they go through that ludicrous charade of trying to change our minds back again.'

'That only works if they really wanted to kill you.'

'They do. That's "A" in this application of Lejeune's law. It's called a working hypothesis. When they fail to change our mind, they call up Doc Macpherson. Doc MacP chunters round fastest so that the second we send out a May Day from Myrtle he can be up here with his hypodermic, administering a homeopathic antidote before you can say Nimrod Herring.'

Monica put down her tea cup and raised her hand. From the world beyond the casement window the church clock could be heard striking the half hour. A cock crew and in the distance a motorbike farted unpleasantly up a bucolic hillside.

'Permission to speak,' said Monica.

'Granted,' said Bognor, 'but not for long.'

'It's all fun as theory,' she said, 'but as none of it ever happened I don't see what it's got to do with...well, what it's got to do with anything much actually.'

'Aha!' said Bognor, triumphantly. 'But that is where you're wrong. I woke at two-twenty this morning to find you face down in the loo vomiting your guts out while in the last stages of salmonella poisoning. Or something very much like it. You were barely conscious.'

74

'Don't be silly.'

'I am not being silly. Please hear me out. I immediately phone zero and there is Felix obviously waiting breathlessly by the phone. Then, hey presto, there's a tramping of elephantine feet and enter Norman Bone and the doctor himself. The doctor charges off into the bathroom while Norman waylays me with a bottle of brandy, and doesn't re-emerge until he's hypnotised you into a deep sleep and jabbed you full of some homeopathic gunge.'

'But Simon I don't remember any of this. You must have been dreaming.'

'Exactly as he said.' Bognor spoke exultantly, but he was beginning to be nervous. If Monica really couldn't remember any of what had happened and if she was feeling weak but otherwise well, then what proof could he produce? He was beginning to have an uneasy feeling that *les deux patrons* and the doctor would deny that any of them had been near the room. He took hold of Monica's hands and stared a little frantically into her eyes. She recoiled in alarm. 'He said you wouldn't remember anything. The cunning bastard. But you do, don't you?'

Monica shook her head. 'I'm sorry Simon, but no, I don't remember any of this. Are you sure you're not having me on?'

'Certainly not,' said Bognor. 'It's as true as I'm sitting here, dammit.'

'Well prove it.' She did not say it unpleasantly but rather with an air of sweet reason.

Bognor thought for a moment. Monica had managed things with her customary efficiency. Nothing would be soiled. All would have been flushed away or (he guessed) removed by the doctor. 'The injection!' he said, suddenly. 'He injected you. The question is where?'

'I thought you said this all happened in the bathroom.'

'Don't be ridiculous,' he snapped. 'I mean where on your body. There'll be a mark. Bruising perhaps if he's less than a dab hand with a syringe and he seemed a bit cut to me.

Question is, did he inject you in the arm or the bottom?'

'You may be my husband but you are not inspecting my bottom for hypodermic needle scars. I am going to scream, Simon, really. I think you're going round the bend.'

'All right, all right.' Bognor tried to calm himself, only too well aware that he must do so if he were to have the slightest chance of convincing her. 'Let's look at your right arm first.'

She poured more tea and looked at him as if trying to decide whether or not to emit the threatened scream. Then slowly she pushed up the sleeve of her nightdress and offered her right arm for inspection. Bognor bent over it like a stamp collector cross examining a suspect penny black.

'Aha,' he said, at length, 'I do believe I have it. Just look at that.' He tried to twist her arm so that she could see the miniscule red dot but in the end he had to fetch his shaving mirror so that she could see the reflection in that. She was not impressed.

'It looks like some sort of a bite to me,' she said. 'Maybe a bed bug.'

'Oh, Monica!' Bognor hid his head in his hands. He felt like banging it against the walls but didn't dare for fear of what it might do to Myrtle's very new and exquisite wallpaper.

'Now calm down,' said Monica. 'I'm going to play Lejeune of the Yard. Let us suppose that everything you say is true. That either I was so deliriously ill or so totally hypnotised or amnesiacked by whatever nettle or dandelion based concoction he put into me that I don't remember a thing. Now why should all three of them also deny it happened? They all seem to have behaved in an exemplary fashion. You're suspicious because Felix answered the phone so quickly and because there was a doctor in the house. But they've anticipated that suspicion by telling you that Norman had suffered one of his brain-damaging migraines. So why go back on that perfectly adequate story?'

'Mighty odd coincidence Norman having a migraine just as you're expiring with food poisoning.'

'So?' Monica looked arch. 'So life is full of amazing coincidences. You mustn't be paranoid. There's more cock-up and coincidence in life than conspiracy and immaculate conception. You know that. It's what you're always telling me.'

'Touché.' Bognor got out of bed and lurched over to the window where he stood scratching his back while he stared out at the mist peeling back off the villagescape. 'You may be right. Lying there thinking about it I just thought that the best possible way of really unnerving me was to pretend that none of it ever happened. If you couldn't remember anything then I would start to half believe that I was dreaming.'

'Forget it,' said Monica. 'You can speculate too much. My mind is in neutral. There's no point in discussing the hypothetical when you can check it in the dictionary. Isn't that Berlins?'

'Isaiah?'

'No, dummy, Berlins with an "s". The Lord Justice of Appeal. His monograph on Crime, Punishment, Laws and Asses.'

'Oh.' Bognor seldom failed to be amazed by his wife's erudition. He had never even heard of Lord Justice Berlins, much less his monograph.

'So,' said Monica, 'ring Doctor Macpherson. Tell him that I've come to, seeming very chipper and compos mentis, and ask him to confirm something or other. That I ought to stay in bed this morning for instance. If he denies all knowledge of last night you have one problem. If he doesn't you have another.'

Bognor groaned. 'I hate riddles,' he said. 'I'm beginning to wonder whether he's likely to do either. Am I right in thinking that the modern English village is a hyper-complicated place?'

'Ancient English villages too,' said Monica. 'No change in that respect. I've been telling you that for days. Now phone Macpherson. He'll be in the book which is in the bedside table along with the po and the Gideon's Bible.'

Bognor had noticed them already when doing his usual routine check of the room. He had been surprised to find the Bible and chamber pot and could only suppose that they had been left over from the previous regime. Neither of them quite tied in with Felix and Norman.

'Macpherson, Dr E. St G.,' he read. 'That's him. I remember the initials on the side of his bag.'

He got an outside line and dialled the number. After a long wait a receptionist answered. 'Dr Macpherson's in Surgery,' she said. 'Can I help?'

Bognor explained that it was urgent. Dr Macpherson had attended his wife in the small hours and he needed immediate advice now that she had regained consciousness. The receptionist asked him to wait and he was treated to a barrage of clicking sounds until Macpherson came on the line sounding neutral if a trifle harassed.

'Macpherson,' said Macpherson.

'Doctor, my wife has come round now and seems quite well.' Bognor chanced his arm, risking a scream from Monica, 'it's just that she and I have a quite different recollection of exactly what you wanted her to do. I thought you wanted her to stay in bed at least for a morning but she distinctly recollects your telling her to get out into the fresh air as soon as possible.'

There was another long pause and although there were no audible clicks Bognor had a distinct sense of cerebral cogs clunking and whirring inside the doctor's head.

'I'm surprised she can remember anything at all about last night,' he said at last. 'She was quite unwell. Delirious in fact. And with the treatment and everything else...ah...perhaps I'd better speak to her myself.'

'Of course.' Bognor handed the phone to his wife who mouthed something unintelligible at him. Not something very agreeable.

'Good morning, Doctor,' she said. 'My husband says I'm to stay in bed this morning.'

Macpherson, though polite enough, sounded mildly put out, and unsure of himself.

'How are you feeling?' he asked. He seemed reluctant even to commit himself to such an anodyne question.

'Fine,' said Monica. 'A bit washed out.'

'Then I think it might be as well if you took it easy. If there are any problems please call me. And if I might offer a word of warning do heed the chef's advice in future. I understand Norman Bone warned you there might be something wrong with the steak.'

'Yes,' said Monica. 'Thanks.'

She replaced the receiver.

'Sorry I doubted you,' she said. 'There is something odd going on.'

'How do you know?' asked Bognor. 'Intuition?'

'Not entirely,' she said. 'I suppose it's not conclusive but I am right in thinking that Felix was extremely persuasive about your having the steak?'

'That's what I've been saying.'

'And exactly the reverse when it turned out that I was going to eat it?'

'Precisely,' said Bognor. 'They were happy enough to murder me, but they baulked at you.'

'You can't prove that, of course,' she said, thoughtfully. 'They might have been telling the truth. Norman might only have realised the rest of the steak was a bit niffy *after* he'd dished up yours. They might have warned you off anyway.'

'But Felix started being peculiar as soon as you said you were having it,' said Bognor. 'The charade about Norman sniffing out the other steaks only came later. It was their number two ploy.'

'And number three ploy,' said Monica, 'was to phone the doctor and get him to come steaming round with the antidote. Again I doubt that would have happened if you'd been the victim. He'd have got here just too late.'

'You can't prove that.' Bognor frowned. 'Even though I'm almost certain you're right.'

'Too much hypothesis and intuition,' agreed his wife. 'But that's what would have happened. Just as well you're not the only carnivorous greedy pig in this family.'

They sipped their Earl Grey with sanguine expressions, contemplating the awfulness that might have been, he a quite ordinary little man in striped pyjamas, she a strapping equine figure in a Marks and Spencer nightie. Neither in the first flush of youth, but both too young to die.

And then, just as it so often did in the aftermath of crisis, the telephone rang. It was ever thus in Bognor's life. There was never a trough between the waves. They kept on coming like Zulus at Rorke's Drift, and whenever the enemy paused to re-group he had to field an attack from his own side.

He gazed sourly at the strident interruptor of their post-almost-mortem. He would know that ring anywhere – more hectoring, more shrill, more insistent than any other telephone call in the world. Always later at night, always earlier in the morning, always inconvenient, as distinctive as the mating call of the grebe or the hunting cry of the stoat.

Parkinson.

Glumly he put the receiver to his ear and said, 'Myrtle here.'

'Oh, come along, Bognor,' His boss's rasping tones grated across the wires from Whitehall. 'It's too early for fun and games and I'm perfectly certain that the lady with you is your lovely wife. Now, Bognor, I want you to take your mind off toast and marmalade and concentrate on what I have to say. Customs and Excise have just been on and...'

When you have worked in intelligence as long as a man like Bognor you develop any number of sixth and seventh senses which enable you to react to circumstances in a man ner which would elude most armchair investigators. It is this which keeps men like Bognor alive: the awareness that the smiling stranger in the Burton suit has knuckledusters on his fingers; that the man with the firm handshake and unflinching stare is shiftier than he seems; above all that walls have ears. Or, more particularly, telephones. For most people the phone seems a private even intimate form of communication into which the most embarrassing intimacies can be communicated. Not to Bognor. In some countries, naturally, he only ever used public call boxes just as he would never do more than pass the time of day in a hotel bedroom unless the taps were running. In Herring St George he might not normally have entertained such suspicions but this was not a normal time and he suddenly – intuitively, if you insist – became aware that there was a third party on the line. And the third party was not there by accident.

'Hang on a sec, sir,' he said. 'I can't hear you very well. I'll call back in a jiffy.'

But Parkinson was being obtuse. 'Our American cousins have come up with some interesting material on your friends the Contractors. A company owned by them's under investigation...'

Stupid oaf, Bognor said to himself. 'Please sir,' he said out loud, 'I'm going to have to call you back...' He cracked the receiver back into its cradle. 'Deskbound Wally!' he said. 'You can tell he's never been out in the field. He's more danger to the country than Philby himself. Utterly crass. He must realise this isn't a secure line. Either Felix or Norman were definitely listening in and in view of what happened last night I only hope I hung up in time.'

'Depends how long he went on talking after you'd put the machine down,' said Monica.

Bognor was getting dressed rapidly, pulling on his Y-fronts and a 'fug' of string vest and shirt, the one encased in the other. 'Where the hell did I put my electric razor?' he asked irritably, 'Did you nick it?'

'What I mean,' said Monica equably refusing to be insulted, 'is that you don't break the connection just by putting the receiver down in your hotel room. The connection is with the switchboard downstairs. So if Parkinson went on talking your eavesdropper would have been able to hear every word he said.'

'Oh, hell!' Bognor was knotting his lurid Arkwright and Blennerhassett Society tie, one of his few remaining links with university life so long ago. 'You're absolutely right. And the way the old fool was blathering on he could have continued for hours committing Christ knows what sort of indiscretion.' He located the razor under his hastily discarded pyjama bottoms and switched on, buzzing cursorily across the stubble of his jowls and chins. 'Whatever he was saying will be all round Herring St George by now,' he said. 'And the crowning absurdity is that practically the only person who's not in on the secret is me.' He peered with displeasure at his reflection in the mirror. 'Sometimes,' he said, wearily, 'I don't think I'm me at all. Where did that sprightly youth go to? What happened to that boundless promise?'

'You were never sprightly,' said Monica harshly. 'What are you going to do?'

'Find a phone box,' he said. 'Call Parkinson and then pay one or two social visits beginning with the intriguing if unlikely Emerald Carlsbad. Something tells me she is up to no good. I shall almost certainly pay my respects also to the maharishi, Phoney Fred. I'll be back in time for a light lunch. Light for you anyway. You're not allowed anything to drink until the sun is over the yard arm. Doctor's orders.'

He pecked her on both cheeks.

'Try to sleep,' he said. 'And if Parkinson calls again, hang up.'

She picked up *The Times* and the Portfolio card.

'See you later,' she said. 'Take care.'

The morning was hazily beautiful as only an English morning in an olde village knows how. Bognor had seen Anne Hathaway's cottage lovingly recreated in exact replica in a garden on Vancouver Island. He had seen an English hamlet with a water mill of genuine English stone in the middle of alligator-infested swamp in Orlando, Florida. He had seen the sunrise over a beach in Mauritius and the Sangre de Cristo mountains of northern New Mexico. But you couldn't beat the real McCoy: the mellow yellow stone, the flutter of butterflies, the skilfully posed roses, the hollyhocks chock-a-block in the little cottage gardens, the sweet peas and the bees, the hives half hidden in the trees, clumps of chives, and parsley and thyme in tubs by low front doors, and there by the wicket gate into the churchyard the scarlet of Victorian pillar box and the village telephone kiosk.

'You can't beat England!' said Bognor, and hummed the first few bars of 'Sussex-by-the-Sea', as he strode bouncily across the green, speckled with buttercup and daisy. No matter how it was traduced and bowdlerised by city interlopers there was something about an English village like Herring St George which could never be destroyed.

He opened the door of the phone box. Even the smell was ancient and traditional – that compound of old sock, manure, last year's cigarettes and ale. The phone had not even been vandalised, as it would have been in any of the country's great conurbations. The graffiti, especially the Swastikas and the 'Pakis go home' suggested interloping Hell's Angels or National Frontiersmen from Whelk and the world outside, but there were still a few 'Kilroy was here's and 'Bill loves Mary's together with cupid's hearts which recalled an earlier, simpler era. For a moment Bognor stood breathing in the unventilated air of a forgotten England and assimilating the sights of a vanished world. Then he dialled the operator, contacting her at only the third attempt, and asked for a reverse charge call to the Board of Trade.

'What the hell are you playing at?' asked Parkinson

angrily, when they had made contact. 'First of all we get cut off and then when I finally get through again your wife refuses to speak to me. Have you gone off your rocker?'

Bognor was very patient. 'I'm afraid,' he said, when this display of Parkinsonian petulance was over, 'that it's not safe to talk on the phones to the Pickled Herring. I've good reason to believe that the proprietors attempted to murder me last night and were only foiled because Monica insisted on eating my steak.'

Parkinson appeared to be experiencing some respiratory trouble.

'Anyway,' continued Bognor, 'I won't bother you with that except to say that in future, don't call me, I'll call you. Now you were in the middle of telling me something that the Americans had discovered about the Contractors.'

'I told you that before we were cut off.'

Bognor winced. 'I'm afraid not, sir. We were cut off before you got to the crucial passage.'

For the first time a shadow of doubt seemed to have crept into Parkinson's voice.

'Odd,' he said. 'I told you all about the company and this chap Herring being the president. I only heard the click and the dialling tone after I'd finished and you didn't reply.'

Bognor suddenly felt queasy.

'What chap Herring being president of what company?'

'Sir Nimrod Herring, Baronet, MC,' said Parkinson. 'President of this Miami registered company called Dull Boy Productions. It seems to be a nominal position because the chief executive is your friend Peregrine Contractor and all the money obviously comes from them. Or I should say "originally came from". Now it's a case of "goes to". The papers are ambiguous to put it mildly; but there's evidently a lot of money in it.'

'Well it's not going to Sir Nimrod,' said Bognor. 'He's as poor as a church mouse. Runs the village shop. Scarcely got two pennies to his name.'

'Don't bank on it, Bognor.' His chief had that knowing

inflection in his voice which meant he was about to teach his subordinate how to suck eggs.

'I don't know how many millionaires you've met in your life, Bognor,' he said, 'but I've known one or two and they're not like you and me.' Bognor resented being thus bracketed with his superior. He felt no affinity with him whatever. But he kept quiet. 'Some of the richest men in the world,' continued Parkinson, 'make a fetish out of appearing not just ordinary but positively down and out. Your Sir Nimrod may well come into precisely that category. Eccentrics are seldom more eccentric than English eccentrics and things are seldom what they seem. I shouldn't have to tell you that, Bognor.'

'Indeed not, sir. You're suggesting then, sir, that Sir Nimrod Herring is a sort of mute inglorious Robert Maxwell.'

'I'm not suggesting anything, Bognor. I'm simply asking you to exercise rat-like cunning and extreme scepticism. Not to say caution.'

'Very well sir.'

Bognor replaced the phone quite gently and then very deliberately kicked the metal wall of the box several times, hard enough to be painful. 'Bloody, bloody, bloody man!' he said, and then repeated, 'Bloody man!' Only then did he feel sufficiently calm to venture back into the world outside.

Herring and Daughter, Village Stores, was on the side of the green between the Pickled Herring and St George's church. It was not a very prepossessing edifice, having been erected in rather a hurry after its predecessor, a thatched sixteenth-century building, had been flattened by one of Hitler's bombs in 1942. The pilot had, it was assumed, jettisoned a surplus one while returning from a raid on the marshalling yards in Whelk. It was the only bomb to fall on Herring St George during the entire conflict.

Bognor pushed open the door and saw at once that his wife was right. The stores were virtually derelict save in the matter of gumboots. They must have acquired a job lot from army surplus. Hundreds hung from the ceiling, mostly but not all in pairs. And on closer inspection he could see that the pairs did not all match. There was a post office counter surrounded by very old admonitory posters and placards advising people to post early for Christmas and make sure they had dog licences but other than that there seemed to be little but a great many cases of Grape-Nuts and a side of bacon sitting on an antique slicer. This last, and the bacon too come to that, looked as if it had been salvaged from the war-time bombing.

A bell tinkled as Bognor entered and a moment later there was some scuffling off and Naomi Herring advanced wearily on the bacon counter. She did not look at all well and Bognor guessed that the unwonted excesses of yesterday's Clout had left her with a hangover. She was wearing a grubby smock similar to, but not identical with, the one she had worn yesterday. Bognor suspected that yesterday's had been her Sunday best.

'Oh, Mr Bognor,' she said. 'It is Mr Bognor isn't it?'

Bognor confirmed that it was.

'What can I do for you?' she asked, smiling rather dourly. She was not a very attractive person with her suet face made whiter yet by an over-generous application of what looked like talcum powder which failed to obscure the unhealthy mauve bags under the eyes. Still, thought Bognor, she had obviously had a sad life; and if she lived on nothing but breakfast cereal it was scarcely surprising if she looked a little pasty. He wondered if he ought to order a pair of boots just to show willing but decided against.

'As a matter of fact I was rather hoping to catch your father.' Bognor smiled feebly, hoping to soften the blow of not being a prospective customer. If only they had sold postcards he would have bought one. It was the mark of really dramatic incompetence to run a shop in such a picture postcard village as Herring St George and yet not actually sell them. He bet you could buy them in Whelk.

'I'm awfully sorry but Daddy's gone off somewhere,' she

said. 'He said he'd be back later. Can I take a message?'
It was curious to hear such Sloane Rangerish language
emanating from such a Mummerset figure. She said 'gawn'
for 'gone', just as her father had called journalists
'jawnalists'. Odd.

'You don't know where he went I suppose?'

'Haven't the foggiest I'm afraid,' said Naomi flicking
a fly off the bacon. 'You're the umpteenth person who's
asked this morning. There's nothing wrong is there?'

'No,' said Bognor, wishing it were true.

'It's not his London day,' she said. 'That's not till next
week. I checked. It's not like him to go charging off like
that. He didn't finish his tea.'

'London day?' Bognor tried to sound nonchalant. 'Does
he often go to London?'

'As regular as clockwork,' said Sir Nimrod's daughter.
'Every third Monday of the month. He has lunch with a
couple of old army friends. At his club.'

She caught the scepticism on Bognor's face, and said,
'He has a country membership, I think. It's terribly cheap.'
She laughed bleakly, 'Maybe it's means tested. I never dared
ask. And I think the others pay for lunch. They should.
They're both Lloyd's underwriters.'

'I see.' Bognor's hand went instinctively to the crown of
his scalp. 'Any idea when he might be back?'

'He just said he'd be back later. He's very vague about
time these days.'

'Did he seem all right? Not agitated in any way?'

Naomi considered for a moment. Bognor watched. It
seemed to cost her a lot of effort. He searched for any
family resemblance but could catch none. Perhaps she was
her mother's child. He must call on the Macphersons and
have a word with them both. Especially Edith.

'To be absolutely honest,' she said, after a lot of screw-
ing up her nose and rubbing her chin, 'he hasn't really been
himself since that odious little VAT inspector came smarm-
ing round. I mean I don't wish to speak ill of the dead but

87

he really was an odious little man. And he was fearfully rude to Daddy. I mean I know my father's not the most methodical person and goodness knows nor am I but we do try and we're not dishonest. If there's anything wrong then it's an honest mistake. But the way he went on you'd think we'd stolen the crown jewels or smuggled in a lorry-load of heroin from Afghanistan. I can't think why he isn't out catching criminals.'

'He isn't out catching anything at the moment,' said Bognor. 'He's in the morgue.'

'Oh, I know, it's rotten luck and all that.' She flicked another fly off the slab, which looked like marble and perhaps therefore much the same as Wilmslow's present resting place as he waited for the forensic surgeon to set about him. 'But if anybody had it coming to him it was Wilmslow. I know it's an unpleasant job but he could have been polite. He really went out of his way to antagonise the whole village. Not just us. Everyone.'

'In what way exactly?'

'Oh his manner more than anything. He told Daddy that it was unpatriotic to be so slovenly over accounting. And when Daddy said he'd fought the Kaiser and Hitler to make life possible for little runts like Wilmslow, Wilmslow said he might have got a commission in the cavalry but he certainly wouldn't have got one in the pay corps. I ask you. The cheek of it.'

'Mmmm.' Bognor conveyed sympathy though he could well imagine that Sir Nimrod would be an irritating customer for a VAT inspector to have to deal with. Having seen the pitiful attempts to complete a VAT return he could well understand that incompetence of that magnitude coupled with the truculence of which he knew the old squire to be capable would have made a nicer man than Wilmslow impatient. 'I'm sorry to trouble you Miss Herring,' he said, 'but when your father does get back I wonder if you could ask him to give me a call? I'm at the Pickled Herring. My room's Myrtle. My wife Monica will take a message.'

Naomi Herring nodded brightly. 'I'll tell Daddy to ring Myrtle in Monica as soon as he gets back,' she said.

'Oh, what the hell,' he thought to himself. There was no point in contradicting a girl like that. She was old enough to be his elder sister which, as he knew to his cost, was too old to change for the better.

Time, he decided, to go and see Emerald Carlsbad, authoress of *Freudian Traumdeutung in the Cook Islands* at her home, the New Maltings. The house, he had already established, was about half a mile past the church on the road to Herring All Saints. It being sunny he would walk, even though it was uphill. The high banked hedgerows were pink and white with dog rose and Queen Anne's lace and a whole lot of other pretty things he was ashamed not to be able to identify. He had done no botany at school. Once or twice he had to flatten himself against the side of the lane as a tractor or horsebox sped past. Country people seemed to drive more recklessly than townees but they did wave very cheerily. Just beyond the churchyard a stout black and white bitch which looked like a cross between a dalmatian and a cocker spaniel came and sniffed rudely at his flies. An acrid smell which he thought might be chicken dung overlay the grass and wild flowers. It was not silage or cow manure, both of which were richer, deeper, browner smells. This was more of an oboe smell where the others were bassoons.

He was sweating when he reached the New Maltings and was using a switch of cow parsley to beat off marauding insects attracted to the perspiration which ran down from his temples and stained his shirt under the arms. He hoped Miss Carlsbad might be prevailed upon for a glass of iced water. This walking about in the country was all very well but it did dry out the throat.

The main part of the house was of ochre stone and dated, he guessed, from around the end of the seventeenth century. Much more recently, however, someone had built on a new wing in white clapboard. Also a rather elegant conservatory which looked as if it had been built to a Victorian design only with modern materials. There was a rather imposing front door at the end of a short path behind a wrought-iron gate; and a more welcoming back door leading off a yard which contained garage and stabling. He was wondering which one to choose when the back door opened and a figure with skin-tight black trousers, a black shirt, and long very shiny black hair emerged clutching a bulky folder of the sort favoured by fashion models carrying round a portfolio of self-portraits. Bognor recognised Damian Macpherson.

'Hello!' he said. 'It's Damian, isn't it? Simon Bognor, Board of Trade. Is Miss Carlsbad at home?'

Damian fingered the stud in his left ear lobe nervously and grinned rather sheepishly. The two met at the back gate.

'Yeah,' said Damian.

'Been in for a spot of therapy then?' enquired Bognor, conversationally. He had not expected to find the doctor's teddy boy son up here, and was intrigued.

'Wot?' said Damian.

'Therapy,' repeated Bognor. 'I understand Miss Carlsbad is by way of being a bit of a therapist. *Freudian Traumdeutung* and all that.'

Macpherson junior looked at Bognor as if he was simple.

''Scuse me guv,' he said in a bizarre pastiche of cockney muddled in with rural English and BBC/public school/Oxford, 'I'm in a bit of an 'urry.' As he uttered these curious words in accents which Bognor had never previously encountered, he made to open the gate. This meant that he was holding his large and unwieldy folder under one arm only. He might well have negotiated this tricky manoeuvre were it not for the fact that at precisely the moment that he tried to open the gate Bognor did the same. For a moment there was a hopeless 'After you Claud, no after you Rodney' as the gate swung this way and that, and then, inevitably, the folder slipped from Damian's grasp and fell to the ground.

'Shit!' said Damian.

'Don't worry,' said Bognor, stooping to retrieve the contents. Very few of the pictures actually fell out of their container but each one of the dozen or so which did were unquestionably of naked females in suggestive poses. And when Bognor picked one up he was transfixed. He could not swear to the rest of her, but the face, softly pouting with shiny lips half open to reveal pearly teeth and the tip of a coral tongue, was unquestionably that of his erstwhile hostess, Samantha Contractor, for once not even in lingerie. It took Damian only a few seconds to scoop the other pictures back into the folder. Then he turned to Bognor who was staring at Samantha's full colour, full frontal picture with amazement.

'Gimme that!' said the Herring St George teddy boy, snatching it from Bognor's grasp. And he shot off out of the yard, clutching his photographs in both hands. Moments later Bognor heard a motorbike kick into action and roar throatily down the hill towards the village.

'Well, well,' he said, 'I wonder what I'm supposed to make of that?'

He stood briefly, scratching his head, and then became aware that a short stout woman with an Eton crop was regarding him from the back doorway with extreme disfavour. Three snuffling pug dogs grizzled at her feet and she held a garden fork in both hands across the body rather as a soldier holds a rifle preparatory to lungeing at a sack with his bayonet.

'Yes?' she said.

'I'm from the Board of Trade,' said Bognor.

'I'm sorry,' said the woman, 'but I never buy at the door. Can't you read?' She gestured to a sign at the side of the door which said, 'No hawkers. No circulars. Beware of the dogs.'

'No,' said Bognor, 'I'm not selling anything. I'm from the Board of Trade.'

'I shall call the police if you don't go away at this

moment. And I warn you that these dogs may look small but they are extremely fierce.'

'Miss Carlsbad, I... '

'I suppose you bought my name from American Express,' she snapped. 'Never a day goes by without one of those insulting personalised invitations but I never expected salesmen to arrive in person. What company do you represent young man? I shall be making a full report.'

Despite the compliment of being referred to as 'young man' Bognor felt, in all conscience, that he was too old to be treated like this even by stout Freudian ladies in brogues and Eton crops. He produced his Board of Trade identity card, advanced on her and flourished it under her nose. The pugs growled liquidly, like canine garglers, but made no move to attack.

'My name is Simon Bognor of the Board of Trade,' he said, 'and I am investigating the death of Mr Brian Wilmslow.'

Miss Carlsbad read the card and then looked up at him, beaming. 'But of course you are, dear boy.' Her mood seemed to have undergone a dramatic transformation. 'Why ever didn't you say?'

Bognor did not know the correct response to this. It was certainly not in any of the training manuals. There seemed no point in arguing about it. So he merely smiled vapidly and asked if he might have a quiet word. It seemed, suddenly, that there was nothing the lady would like more. She prodded her dogs indoors with her fork, and seizing Bognor by the arm, propelled him in after them.

'What a lot of fuss about a VAT inspector!' she exclaimed. 'I've already had a very handsome policeman asking questions. Rather dull questions it has to be said, which was a pity when he was so good looking.' She kicked at one of the pugs. 'Go away Randolph, sir!' she exclaimed. Then turned back to Bognor. 'Would you like to sit outside by the pool or indoors?'

Bognor said he'd like to sit out by the pool as it was such

a lovely day and she told him to take off his jacket and would he like a glass of something cold and he did say his name was Bognor didn't he and did that mean that everybody made the same boring old remark about George V's famous last words. Bognor took off his jacket and said 'Yes please', 'Yes' and 'Yes'.

'That's settled then,' said Miss Carlsbad enigmatically, when they were seated in slatted chaise longues by the side of a new kidney-shaped swimming pool by the conservatory. 'Now how can I help you? I have to tell you I hardly knew Mr Wilmslow. He called only once and asked exceedingly silly questions about money.'

'That was his job,' said Bognor, sipping a very welcome glass of iced lemonade which Miss Carlsbad claimed to have made herself.

Miss Carlsbad took the spectacles from the top of her pepper and salt Eton crop and moved them to the end of her slightly squashed almost pugilistic nose. They had thick lenses and were secured to her neck by thick black elastic.

'I guessed it,' she said and chirruped with bird-like laughter. 'Money, money, money. But you and I are not going to talk about money Mr Bognor, although I would prefer it if you changed your name. We are going to talk about death. Death.' She rolled the word around her lemon barley water as if by repeating it she might actually kill someone or something. She seemed peeved when no corpse materialised.

'Yes,' said Bognor. 'Do you have any idea at all why Mr Wilmslow should have been killed?'

Miss Carlsbad scrutinised him for a moment. Then she said, 'I don't call that much of a question. Ask me another.'

Bognor grinned. 'Do you know why anyone should want to kill Mr Wilmslow?' he tried.

'Better,' she said. 'I'd say that anyone who goes round asking impertinent questions about people's financial affairs was asking for trouble. That's reasonable enough wouldn't you say? Ask me another.'

'Would you have killed him – given the opportunity?'

Miss Carlsbad laughed again. The same fluting birdsong. 'That's a very bold question for so early in our interview. But more interesting than being asked what one was doing last night and having to answer that one was watching television with the dogs and then going to bed with a good book. Well, not such a good book I'm afraid. I was under the misapprehension that it was about a parrot but it isn't at all. Gerald Durrell is quite one of my favourite authors, and I'm fond of birds. I may build an aviary one day when my boat comes in.' She beamed.

'You didn't answer the question.'

'What was it?'

'Would you have killed Mr Wilmslow given the opportunity.'

'I think that question is both hypothetical and leading and so if you don't mind I prefer not to answer it. Pass.'

Bognor drank deep from his glass and frowned. This sort of interrogation was so difficult. In the books he would have taken Miss Carlsbad down to the basement of the Board of Trade, injected her with some truth serum and hit her about with an electric cattle prod. If you believed the books the British were no better than the KGB or even the Argies. In Bognor's experience this was not the case. He was barely allowed even to ask a trick question. As for hitting anybody about...

'Miss Carlsbad, it may be that Mr Wilmslow's death was accidental. On the face of it, it looks as if it might have been. Nevertheless he was in the course of conducting some very delicate enquiries in Herring St George and therefore my colleagues and I do naturally have some suspicions.'

'Just what your colleague said, Mr Bognor,' Miss Carlsbad looked sympathetic. 'I quite understand.'

'VAT inspectors have considerable powers,' said Bognor. 'They can search your house and take away all your papers without so much as a "by your leave". Prising out people's guilty secrets is their stock in trade.'

Miss Carlsbad nodded, a little primly this time.

'In view of what happened to Mr Wilmslow,' he said, 'I think perhaps we should stop beating about the bush.' He paused as a heavy vehicle which sounded like a tank transporter but was probably a mere combine harvester thundered up the hill drowning speech as effectively as Concorde on its Heathrow approach over his home in west London. 'In other words,' he said, leaning forward and speaking with that slight air of melodrama which − it seemed to him − was part of Miss Carlsbad's stock in trade, 'what exactly is *your* guilty secret?'

One of the pugs pushed at Bognor's trouser leg and he flinched as he felt the clammy little nose on his calf. 'Get off, Winston!' said Miss Carlsbad kicking at the dog half-heartedly. 'Now that, if I may say so Mr Bognor, is an exceedingly leading question. You don't really expect me to answer it do you?'

'Listen, Miss Carlsbad,' said Bognor, in the frank, matter of fact, I'm only trying to help, tone which he often adopted with older women, 'if you have a guilty secret and by "guilty" I only mean something which you personally feel embarrassed by then there are two ways in which I can discover it. One is by you telling me straight out and the other is by an exhaustive and exhausting series of enquiries which will involve searches and interviews with your bank manager and heaven knows what else besides. Now I draw my salary no matter which course we adopt so it's really no skin off my nose. But in your case...' He allowed the unpleasant prospects to hang in the air, all the more threatening for their lack of precision.

'When you say "guilty secret", Mr Bognor, I wonder if you could be a little more precise.' Miss Carlsbad smiled frostily. Bognor was glad, suddenly, that he was not a patient of hers. No fun at all to be lying on her couch with her beady Freudian eyes boring into you. He wondered what the Cook islanders had made of her.

'That's rather a chicken and egg question. If I knew what

the secret was I could be more specific. Since I don't – yet – I'm compelled to be vague. Sorry.'

'Then I'm not sure I can help.'

Bognor sighed. 'Listen,' he said again. 'As far as we are able to determine at this moment in time...' Why was he speaking like a Wilmslow he asked himself irritably? It was not in character. It must be the effect of Miss Carlsbad. 'As far as I can see,' he corrected himself, 'you have two declared sources of income. One is from your books and one is from your therapy. Now I doubt very much that the income which appears in your VAT returns could possibly be accounted for by any therapy you do and I'm absolutely certain it can't be explained by the royalties from Freudian whatsit in the Cook Islands.'

'*Traumdeutung*,' said Miss Carlsbad.

'*Traumdeutung*,' agreed Bognor. He waved his hand to encompass the pool, the conservatory, the gardens, Miss Carlsbad's rather beautiful house. 'You can't tell me two volumes of South Pacific psychiatry...'

'...ology,' said Miss Carlsbad.

'...ology,' he said testily, 'paid for all this.'

'You want to know where the money comes from,' said Miss Carlsbad.

'In a word, yes.'

'Well,' Miss Carlsbad stared into the limpid waters of her kidney-shaped swimming pool, 'it makes a change from being asked where I spent last night. You'd better come inside.'

They entered through french windows and passed through a long airy drawing room furnished in various shades of cream. He noticed a couple of signed Pipers, a Hockney and something that looked suspiciously like a blue period Picasso. In one corner caught perfectly by the morning sun was a bronze Boadicea which had a definite air of Frink and if he didn't know what it must have cost he could have sworn the small entwined couple on the coffee table surrounded by *Interiors* and *House and Garden* and *Country Life* was a Henry Moore. He was impressed, and even more curious.

After that there was a dining room with a suite which looked as if it was at least school of Sheraton decorated with Venetian scenes which were at least school of Guardi; then a Poggenpohl kitchen; a hall and, at last, their destination. This was in the original part of the house. It was a beamed room with bookcases all round the walls except for the fireplace (full of bright flowers dried the previous summer) and a bread oven in one corner. On the desk top was a very new IBM personal computer.

'He's transformed my life that little fellow,' said Miss Carlsbad. 'I used to dictate into a machine like Ba Cartland but I never really liked it. It was fast but it was soulless. I like to see the words on screen or paper. Somehow they're not real otherwise.'

Bognor was foxed. He looked up at the shelves. Freud, Jung, Adler – volume after volume in what looked like original editions – and then ranged alongside book after book of what critics and commentators had written about Freud, Jung and Adler.

'Well,' said Miss Carlsbad, 'this is it. You're very privileged. It's rare indeed for anyone else to penetrate my little word factory.'

'I see,' said Bognor, without really thinking.

'No you don't,' she said. 'There's no money in that. One day I will publish *Freudian Traumdeutung in an English Village* but it will be no more of a money maker than the Cook Islands. Over here, dear boy,' and she moved him across to the far shelves. 'This is my stuff. Cast your eye down this shelf here and see if you can solve the little riddle. No one else has but then I don't really have that sort of public. More's the pity. See if you can solve it, while I get some more lemonade. Unless you'd like something stronger. I can add a little vodka if you'd prefer.'

Bognor looked at his watch and said no thank you very

much he was trying to cut out booze before noon.

'Very sensible,' she said. 'If only your friend Mr Wilmslow had steered clear of the demon drink he might be with us today.' Bognor looked at her sharply when she said that. The fact that Wilmslow was paralytic with drink was not supposed to be public knowledge but then as Bognor was beginning to realise the Herring St George grapevine was as effective as any communications network he had ever come across. He didn't see how Miss Carlsbad or anyone else could possibly have kept her secret. But then, he thought, perhaps she hadn't kept it from her fellow villagers. Perhaps there were no secrets among the villagers. Perhaps it was just that the villagers kept their secrets to themselves, collectively. In which case Wilmslow was on a hiding to nothing. And he and Guy Rotherhithe as well.

He turned to the shelf, determined to unravel its secret. He removed the first volume, the one at the extreme left. It had been published in 1951 and was called *Roves back the Rose*, by Emerald A. Trawle. He began to read the first page:

'An icy chill spread through me. "Are you ill?" I whispered. He smiled, a thin shadow of that gay smile which I remembered so vividly from last summer, that Oh so blissful summer at Fotheringay. "It's the side effects," he said, "of the..." He could say no more. 'You mean it's cancer?' He nodded. 'Inoperable. The doctor says I have a month. Six weeks at most...'

Bognor smiled. Jolly lucrative stuff this. It explained everything. Emerald A. Trawle was Emerald Carlsbad's bodice-ripping pseudonym. He ran his eye hurriedly along the shelf. She was nothing if not prolific. *Our Dreams are Tales*, *Whisper Awhile*, *The Shades of Araby*, *Where the Princes Ride at Noon*, *Bright Towers of Silence*, *Beauty Passes*, *Assail Mine Eyes*, *All Things Lovely*, *Poor Jim Jay*, *The Silence Surged*, *The Restless Sea*, *The Glow-Worm*

Shine, Dark Hair and Dark Brown Eyes, Worn Reeds Broken, All Words Forgotten, Silver Shoon, The Elder Tree, Lamps of Peace, For Them That Life Forlorn, The Bonnie Ash.

He had not heard her returning footsteps. 'Well,' she asked, 'have you cracked the code?'

Bognor accepted a second lemonade. 'I'm halfway there,' he said. 'Emerald A. Trawle is your nom de plume and this is how you pay for the pool and the paintings.'

'*One* of my pseudonyms, Mr Bognor.' She smiled. 'If you look at the other shelves you'll see a number of others – Matt Durango, for instance: *The Law of the Lariat, Ten Gallon Tootsie, The Man from Truth or Consequence, The End of the Trail*...and Earl J. Tuxedo: *Cache in Connecticut, Treasure in Texas, Murder in Michigan, Rhode Island Red* – but I'm fondest of Emerald. She was the first and she's much the cleverest.'

'An anagram,' said Bognor. 'Hang on.' He got out his diary and scribbled 'Emerald A Trawle' in capital letters vertically one above the other, the way he always did when grappling with an anagrammatical crossword clue:

E
M
E
R
A
L
D
A
T
R
A
W
L
E

'Well,' he said, frowning, 'Trawle is "Walter" isn't it?'

Miss Carlsbad nodded. 'Now you really are almost there. Emerald A.'

Bognor screwed up his face in a spasm of concentration. 'De la Mare,' he said, triumphantly, 'Walter de la Mare.'

Miss Carlsbad clapped her hands. She seemed genuinely chuffed. 'That's good, Mr Bognor, very good. Do you know de la Mare's work?'

'Not really since school,' he said. 'I prefer something a bit crisper and more modern. Gavin Ewart, for instance.'

'He's rather rude,' said Miss Carlsbad disapprovingly. 'For my taste that is. I don't like this modern preoccupation with physical detail. I'm not a prude but I do think some things are best left to the imagination. Don't you?'

Bognor did not wish to get embroiled in an argument about eroticism and pornography, though he did wonder if Miss Carlsbad had any idea of what young Damian Macpherson had been carrying in his portfolio. He must ask about Damian now that the business of Miss Carlsbad's secret income was resolved. So he said feebly 'Up to a point.'

'Well I wouldn't expect you to guess this,' she said, 'but each one of Emerald's titles is a phrase from a de la Mare poem. They make marvellous titles. Emerald and I are working on "a most beautiful lady". I ask you. What could be a simpler and more perfect title for a romantic novel than that?'

'Very neat,' he said, 'and how long does it take you and Emerald to knock out a finished book?'

'With the computer between a week and ten days,' said Miss Carlsbad beaming, 'but I try not to do more than about twenty titles a year all told. Any more than that and I find that my standards start to slip. And contrary to what is sometimes supposed readers are very discriminating. They notice if you don't give them what they're used to.'

Bognor said he didn't doubt it. 'And what do you make out of it?' he asked.

'A lot,' she said. 'Enough to live very comfortably, as you can see. The figures are all in the accounts. What you won't find is any mention of Emerald and Matt and Earl. But that's my little secret. Isn't it, Mr Bognor?'

'I suppose so,' he said, slightly chastened now. He could see no murder motive in this particular secret. It all seemed perfectly above board.

'I can't see any reason why anyone else should know that you're Emerald Trawle as well as Emerald Carlsbad,' he said, 'nor Matt Durango or Earl J. Tuxedo. Is there anyone else?'

'No one lasting,' she said, 'a number of experiments. What the modern generation might call one-night stands. Such an unpleasant notion. But essentially there are just the three of us and me. I'm sorry, I don't feel I've been of much help in solving the business of poor Mr Wilmslow's death. Was it murder do you suppose? Perhaps it could be a real-life mystery for Earl Tuxedo?'

'I don't know if it was murder,' said Bognor, 'but I'm hoping we'll find out before the day is over. It seems almost certain that he was on to something or someone. Our job is to find out what. It means sifting through all his notes and papers as well, I'm afraid, as talking to everyone he was investigating. Hence this visit.' He drained his lemonade and stood up. 'I'm sorry to have taken up your time, Miss Carlsbad, I hope I won't have to trouble you again.' He moved to the door and then paused as if the thought had only just struck him.

'Damian Macpherson,' he said, but his mind was only half on the subject of the strange doctor's son, fascinating though he found him. 'Is he a friend or a patient or...'

Miss Carlsbad did not seem keen on this question, but suddenly neither did Bognor. 'I'm sorry Miss Carlsbad,' he said, 'but you don't have such a thing as an aspirin? I feel...' he swayed slightly and put a hand to his forehead. 'I think I'll sit down for a second, if you don't mind. Bad night. I...'

Miss Carlsbad seemed relieved at the diversion. 'Shan't be a jiffy,' she said, and hurried out in the direction of her medicine chest. The second she was out of the room Bognor switched on the computer and jammed two floppy disks into the drive. It took only seconds to tap out the instructions for the machine to copy a file from one disk to the other and not much more to remove both disks and put one in his jacket pocket, then subside into an armchair before Miss Carlsbad.

As she came in he was shaking his head. 'I'm terribly sorry,' he said, rubbing his eyes, 'I suddenly came over very queer. I thought I was going to faint. I was up a lot of last night. My wife had a nasty turn and we had to get the doctor.' He accepted the aspirin and a glass of water and hoped she wouldn't notice that he'd been interfering with her computer. If she did she showed no sign of it. She was quite solicitous, wanted to know if he would like to lie down, should she phone Macpherson, call Mrs Bognor.

'No really,' he said, standing gingerly, 'I feel much better already. Can't think what it was.' He grinned ruefully, 'One of life's little warnings I expect. Someone up there telling me to slow down. I have rather a dodgy family history I'm afraid. Bognors don't make old bones. But a good breath of fresh air and a brisk stroll should sort it out for the time being.'

He was relieved to get away with the disk undetected; and she too, he felt, seemed glad to see the back of him. Was he wrong in thinking she was apprehensive about more questions on the subject of Damian Macpherson? Or was she twitchy about having given away only an innocent secret when there was another more guilty one lurking, perhaps in the computer? Bognor felt in his pocket and prayed he might learn something from the purloined disk. Guy would be bound to have a compatible computer he could play it back on.

He wasn't sure if he was getting anywhere or not. He wanted to play the tape, wanted to talk again to Sir

Nimrod, wanted to find out why Damian Macpherson was wandering round with photos of naked ladies, and especially Sam Contractor, wanted to carry out any number of investigations, but right now he decided it was time to call on the swami and his friends.

He was not well disposed towards the swami but he was not sure he regarded him as a prime suspect. It was not that he believed in the swami's pacific protestations. On the contrary, he did not believe in any of the swami's protestations. He seemed to be most things that everyone said but Bognor was man enough to admit that if he had the chance to drive around in a succession of Bugattis waited on hand and foot by adoring girls he would have taken it. He was not a prude. It was just, he felt, that the fates had not dealt him that sort of hand. The fates had dealt him Monica, Parkinson and the Board of Trade, not to mention an unprepossessing physical appearance. He was not complaining. He could have been a lot worse off. But better off too. As well off as Phoney Fred.

It was thoughts such as these which occupied his mind as he strolled along the lane from the New Maltings to Herring Hall. He had never been to Herring Hall before. It was Victorian, built originally for a rich city financier, who had gone broke shortly after moving in. It had then been acquired by an American oil millionaire who had bought it mainly for the shooting. During the first war it had been a convalescent home for the walking wounded and immediately afterwards it was turned into a hotel, with only modest success. In 1939 it was again requisitioned by the army who had originally used it for expatriate Poles and later as a VD clinic.

In 1947 it was taken over by a boys' preparatory school which folded in the late sixties. The National Trust turned it down, an appeal fund foundered before it began, the Bishop of Whelk briefly considered it as a home for distressed diocesan clergy, and then the property developer failed in his efforts to turn it into a Theme Park. It was then that the Chosen Light and his Blessed Followers arrived, cash in hand, and set about restoring it. It had been a chequered career but those who knew about such things said it was in better nick than at any time in its history.

Bognor was looking forward to seeing inside and he was looking forward to meeting Fred. The knowledge that Wilmslow had been looking at Fred's books prior to his demise gave him a goodish excuse. Given the prevailing state of prejudice against organisations such as the swami's he simply had to be at or near the top of any list of suspects. If he went before a jury anywhere in Britain it was highly unlikely that Fred would be acquitted of anything, no matter what evidence was offered. He was too rich, too smelly, too black and too sexy. The man in the street, Clapham omnibus and jury did not like that sort of person. As far as the average Englishman was concerned the swami was a bloody nig-nog taking work from decent people, corrupting the morals of the young, and worst of all having a thoroughly good time.

Bognor was sufficiently self-aware to recognise that what he felt most about Fred was envy. But since he disliked himself for this and since curiosity was running a good second and since, as a government official investigating the mysterious death of another government official, he had a strong hand he was rather looking forward to the visit.

There was a guard at the lodge. A long red pole with a No Entry sign attached to it blocked the drive and alongside stood an olive skinned female who looked as if she had been seconded from an Israeli paratroop commando. She wore jungle green fatigues, dark glasses, and a saffron beret, heavy black boots and white gauntlets. In her right hand she was carrying a cross between a baseball bat and an Indian club. The only indication that she wasn't an Israeli paratrooper was that across her ample bosom was stencilled the single word PEACE. It was this word that she repeated as Bognor hove in sight. To be absolutely accurate what she said was, 'Peace Brother! I am Sister Ra Blessed Follower of the Chosen Light.'

Bognor, who was feeling rather light on his pins, replied, quick as a flash, 'Peace Sister! I am Simon Bognor of the Board of Trade.'

This was obviously not quite such a good idea as it seemed because Sister Ra looked singularly unamused, fixed him with a steely gaze and said 'So?'

'What do you mean "So"?' asked Bognor, aggrieved.

'I mean "so" as in "so what?"' she said. She spoke in an American accent which Bognor, without total certainty, identified as Bronx. He had an idea they were bossy in the Bronx. From the lodge behind her two other guards, similarly dressed, one male one female, emerged twirling sticks.

'What does he want?' asked the male, a big black man with a scar down one cheek.

'He, as you call him, wishes to come in and have words with your swami,' said Bognor, crossly. 'And I'd be obliged if you'd open up and let me in.'

'You have an appointment?' asked the big man, who was evidently in charge.

'As a matter of fact, no,' said Bognor. 'Nevertheless I wish to see the swami.'

'Swami don't see no one without an appointment.'

'Swami see me with or without an appointment,' said Bognor. 'I am a representative of Her Majesty's Government and this is still Her Majesty's country. We do not like private police forces in this country and if I may give you a word of advice I should get through to the swami pretty damn quickly or there could be very serious trouble. There's been one death already and if you don't co-operate I'll have this whole shooting match closed down tomorrow before you can say Hari Krishna.'

Difficult to say why Bognor had become so excited. Something to do with attitudes. Now that he was middle aged he was beginning to find insolence hard to take.

The three Blessed Followers regarded him with mild but broadly unsympathetic interest.

'ID?' said their leader, flatly, holding out a glove.

'ID,' agreed Bognor holding out his laminated Board of Trade special investigator's identity card but prudently not letting go. Like a passport it had some impressive phrases about 'let or hindrance'. It was signed by Her Majesty's Secretary for Home Affairs.

The man turned to the girls, shrugging. 'Where is Fred?' he asked.

The first girl looked at her watch. 'Playing tennis with the Minister for Extra Terrestrial Affairs,' she said. 'Do you want me to call the office?'

'Sure,' said the man, and the paratrooperine unslung a small walkie-talkie from her belt and pressed a sequence of buttons.

'Auntie Ba?' she said. 'Sister Ra on main gate. We have a government inspector here wanting to see the swami.' She paused and glanced at Bognor. 'No not in the least,' she said, 'but he has ID. Just shows, you never can tell. I guess looks aren't everything.' Bognor pretended to ignore this but sucked his stomach in nonetheless. 'Hang about,' said Sister Ra into the machine, 'I'll check.' She looked across at Bognor and said, 'What did you say your name was and your outfit?'

'Simon Bognor,' said Bognor stiffly, 'Board of Trade.'

The girl giggled, but slightly less inimically than before.

'He says Simon Bognor of the Board of Trade,' she said, and then, 'O.K. We'll wait.' She looked across at Bognor and put her hand over the mouthpiece. 'They're calling the swami on the tennis court right now.'

For a minute or two Bognor stood mouthing obscenities to himself, shifting from one foot to the other, and pretending not to ogle the girl soldiers. Then Sister Ra's walkie-talkie came to life again and she listened intently, then put her hand over it again and asked Bognor, 'Were you at Apocrypha College, Oxford, in the early sixties?'

Bognor's jaw did not exactly drop but it felt extraordinarily disconnected. 'Well, yes, as a matter of fact, but what's that got to do with anything?'

Evidently rather a lot because when Sister Ra conveyed the news to Auntie Ba there was an immediate change in attitude and relaxation in tension. The gate was raised, and Sister Ra and the other two smiled quite nicely and bowed their heads. Sister Ra even put down her stick and raised both hands, prayer fashion, to her mouth. Bognor, British to the last, nodded curtly, and said 'Morning.'

'Sister Ra will drive you to the court,' said the man in charge. He seemed somewhat chastened at Bognor's admittance. Sister Ra strode manfully to an old silver Harley Davidson and kicked it into life. 'Get on!' she shouted. 'And hold tight.' He did as he was told and they jolted off down the drive which was in mercifully good order, then swung off down a narrow path, narrowly missing a group of girls in white robes who were either kneeling in prayer or weeding the rosebeds. Ahead was a long high windowless building with a skylight.

An exquisite oriental girl in white was standing by a door. She bowed slightly and raised hands in greeting. 'Mr Bognor, I am pleased to meet you. I am Monday's bride, Blessed Orchid. The swami has almost finished his tennis match but he has asked if you would very much mind sitting with me in the dedans until it is over.'

'The what?'

'The dedans,' said the little girl, tinkling an oriental giggle. 'This is not lawn tennis, Mr Bognor, but real tennis which is the Holy Game of the Blessed Followers of the Chosen Light.'

'I see,' said Bognor.

Inside it was quite dim. Blessed Orchid guided him into a low gallery with rows of benches. From where he sat he could see two men in white flannels. They were holding asymmetrical rackets, not unlike ordinary tennis rackets, steamrollered or mangled. At the net, which was much like a tennis net but which drooped, another bride, a big busty blonde, called out, 'Hazard Chase the Door.'

'Aha,' said Bognor, knowingly, 'this is *real* tennis. I've seen it at Lord's.'

'Ah so,' said Blessed Orchid, 'Lord's is a very holy place. Real tennis is a very holy game!'

The figure who now approached them in their dug-out was very short, rather stout and almost totally unrecognisable on account of the facial hair which enveloped him. You could not say that he was bearded or moustached. He was just covered in hair. As he picked two balls out of the netting which separated him from the spectators he peered into the dedans and smiled at Bognor. 'Hello, Simon,' he said. 'Most awfully good to see you after all these years. This won't take a jiffy and I'll be right with you.'

For a second the years rolled away and Bognor was back on the lawn in Balliol's garden quad playing croquet with a dapper, lean, immaculate Indian lawyer whose ambition was to become his country's Lord Chief Justice.

'Good God!' said Bognor, 'Bhagwan Josht!'

It was the swami's serve at match point. Bognor watched with a curiosity which verged on incredulity. The swami struck the ball from well back in his own half, hitting it with a heavy underhand slice which propelled it up on to a sloping roof to the left hand side of the court. The ball spun off this, striking the black wall at the far end and bouncing back at ankle height and a totally unexpected (to Bognor) angle. The Minister for Extra Terrestrial Affairs did not seem at all perturbed by this for he struck the ball very cleanly and with a low trajectory straight at Bognor's seat. The swami, evidently surprised by this defiance, did not move, and the ball crashed into the netting only inches from Bognor's nose. 'Fifteen forty' called the blonde bride.

'But surely that was out,' said Bognor to Blessed Orchid, but Blessed Orchid only put a finger to her lips and said, 'Shhh.' Once more the swami took a ball from the netting, and cut it hard on to the sloping roof; once more the

Minister for Extra Terrestrial Affairs hit the ball clean and hard but this time it came higher and sailed over the netting. Bognor heard it hit a wall somewhere above him and seconds later it came plopping down tamely, bouncing high so that the swami had time to aim carefully. This time he hit it low over the net to his right where it crashed into the base of an inconveniently situated buttress. As it hit this it came screaming off at right angles straight towards the minister who, miraculously, got his racket to it and managed to return the ball in a high arc out of Bognor's sight.

The swami however obviously had a good sight of it. Bognor could hear it bouncing around above and watched as the swami held his uncouth racket very high above his shoulder, elbow cocked for what he obviously thought was going to be a coup de grâce. As the ball fell and bounced, the swami's racket described a languid swing and the ball sailed off towards the furthest of three netted apertures on the left hand side.

'Clot!' thought Bognor. 'He's hit it out.' But as the ball struck the netting and a little bell tinkled, the swami raised both arms in a boxer's salute and Blessed Orchid cried out, 'Beezer shot Beatitude!' Bognor scratched his head. It was most perplexing. Perhaps the swami made the rules up as he went along.

Outside the swami shook Bognor's hands effusively and introduced him to the Minister for Extra Terrestrial Affairs as a 'very very old friend from university days'. The minister looked suspicious but was swiftly dismissed. So was Orchid. The swami said he would summon her for meditation in an hour or two.

'Come, Simon, old friend,' said the Chosen Light alias Bhagwan Josht alias Phoney Fred. 'We'll wander up to the office and have a chin wag. I suppose you've come about Wilmslow, your colleague. We've had the police here already. Guy Wapping, no less. He didn't recognise me, I'm glad to say. Not surprising, I suppose. We hardly knew each other at Oxford. He struck me as none too bright.'

Two very pretty girls in white robes passed them, bowing very low indeed. The swami reached into his little leather pouch and threw two scraps of purple paper at them. The girls pounced on them and pressed them to their lips with expressions of vapid ecstasy. The swami glanced at Simon.

'You're not to laugh, Simon,' he said. 'These people derive great pleasure from that sort of thing.'

'What are they?' asked Bognor.

The swami shrugged. 'Just pieces of paper soaked in lavender water. I've been using them ever since I started in this business. It's very effective.'

'And just how did you start?'

The swami chuckled. 'I tried the law for a while. Never liked it very much. It was one thing to be at the Inner Temple but frankly it wasn't at all the same thing back home. Then some friends took me down to Poona to see what was going on down there. Honestly, Simon, what a racket! Well, of course, I said to myself, this is the life. So I set up a little ashram and went from strength to strength. It's all a question of marketing!'

They had reached the big house now – a ludicrous red brick schloss on the lines of Keble College and St Pancras station, a preposterous mélange of turret and stained glass, flying buttresses and Gothic archways. Over the porte-cochère hung a vivid saffron banner saying, 'Blessings!'

'Do you mind very much taking your shoes off?' asked Bognor's old friend. 'It's a house rule.'

Bognor didn't mind at all though he was rather self-conscious about the hole in his socks. He wished he could persuade Monica to darn them. The swami obviously had no trouble finding people to darn his socks.

'I'm on the first floor,' he said. 'Shall we walk or take the lift?'

They walked. The main staircase was immensely wide and curved gently upwards from the vast marbled entrance hall. All the better, Bognor supposed, to make your flaunting entrance and exits. It was all show. On the first floor they walked along a long red-carpeted gallery, past a room labelled Communications Centre which was full of gossiping Telex machines and earnest robed men and women staring intently at computer screens.

'If you're competing with people like Rothschilds and the Chase Manhattan,' said the swami, 'you've got to have all the gear.'

'I see,' said Bognor.

At the end of the corridor Bhagwan Josht took a plastic card from his white flannel trousers and pushed it into a slot. The door slid open and he motioned Bognor inside.

'One must have a little privacy,' he said. 'Help yourself to a drink while I have a quick shower and change into something simple.' He showed Bognor into a sumptuous drawing room full of leather furniture. 'Fridge in the bookcase,' said the swami. 'Just press Halsbury's *Laws of England* volume one.'

Bognor did and the books retracted to reveal a large Westinghouse refrigerator full of alcohol. He poured himself a glass of white wine, spent a moment or two studying the pictures of the swami greeting various world leaders. (He particularly liked the one of him giving a piece of purple paper to Mr Andropov; also the one of him and the Queen Mother having a bit of a giggle.) Then he sat down, sifted through the magazines on the table and began to read the *Investors Chronicle*. Presently the swami came in wearing a shining saffron robe and smelling strongly of Fabergé.

'I didn't know you were allowed drink,' said Bognor.

'Oh, we aren't,' said the swami, pouring a Perrier. 'Visitors only. Bad for business not to be able to offer some of our clients a drink.' He sat down. 'Well,' he said, raising his glass, 'chin, chin. Long time no see. How's Monica by the way?'

'She's very well,' said Bognor. 'We're married nowadays. What happened to that tall girl from Lady Margaret Hall you used to knock around with? The one with the cleft chin.'

'I'm told she became a TV personality.' The swami laughed. 'But as you may have deduced I no longer have to worry about that side of things. It's all taken care of. On a rota basis.' He laughed again, slapping his little fat thigh.

'Isn't it all...' Bognor tried to suppress a sharp stab of envy. 'Well ...immoral...I mean shouldn't you be doing something more worthwhile?'

'Like working for the Board of Trade?' The swami laughed quite uproariously this time and pointed mirthfully at his old croquet partner. 'You should see your face!' he said. 'I think you should join up at once. I'll send you the application forms.'

'No but seriously,' said Bognor, chastened, 'I mean...'

'Seriously nothing old boy,' said the swami seriously. 'I run a very tight ship and I do a lot of good. The people who come here are nearly always very unhappy, very lonely, very insecure, and they have no sense of purpose. We change all that. Here they belong to a community. They have friends. We protect them from the unpleasantness of what is laughingly described as civilisation. Nothing wrong with that.'

'And most of them happen to be very rich.'

'There's no means test,' said the swami. 'Not even an admission fee.'

'But there's an overwhelming tendency to take on poor little rich people?'

'There are an awful lot of poor little rich people around these days.' The swami turned up his palms in a gesture of mock despair. 'The other day a man came to me. His family run one of the biggest breweries in South America. He pleaded with me to let him join. Miserable as sin he was. A wreck. Now he works in the greenhouse and thinks I am some sort of god. He's probably crazy but he's happy for the first time in his life. What should I have done? Turned him away?'

'And how much money did he bring?'

'Around fifty million dollars.' The swami shrugged. 'Sure. It's a lot of money. But it's very carefully invested and he gets the benefit.'

'Working in the greenhouse?'

'It's what he wants. Why should I answer.'

'I don't know,' said Bognor. 'It doesn't seem quite right somehow.'

'All communities are the same,' said the swami. 'Many people who have worldly goods are unhappy with them but they can't renounce them altogether. So they make them over to cynics like myself. We look after them and enjoy the loot. The Church has done it for centuries.'

'Oh well,' said Bognor. 'There are some things I shall never understand.'

'That's life,' said the swami, looking profound. 'But it's something I'm afraid your colleague Mr Wilmslow had some trouble understanding.'

'Oh?'

'You knew he'd been to see me?' The swami raised his eyes to the ceiling which was painted by minor Pre-Raphaelites. A Judgement Day scene of peculiar lugubriousness. Bognor often wondered if all Victorians were such whey-faced drips as the PRB made out.

'Yes,' said Bognor. 'He'd been to see everyone in Herring St George of any substance. Anyone that is who was registered for VAT. I'm afraid that includes Sir Nimrod Herring who could hardly be said to be of substance.'

'Yes.' The swami seemed thoughtful. 'Sir Nimrod. I think there may be slightly more to him than meets the eye but I'm afraid his so-called shop isn't much of a success. I had hoped to deal with him in the interests of good community relations. Not possible. In fact, to be perfectly frank, the village is pretty impossible all round. I don't know what the country's coming to. A right lot of faggots and johnny-come-latelies.' Bognor remembered that Bhagwan Josht had been to Harrow. His father had held some minor Indian title. His elder brother still lived in the family palace, crumbling slowly to dust in some God-forsaken northern city where once their word had been law. Bhagwan was better off where he was.

'No, your Mr Wilmslow was a most unpleasant piece of work,' said the swami, 'but not the first we've come across since moving in to Herring St George.' He paused. 'I'll be perfectly frank, Simon, we're not everyone's cup of tea, and partly for that reason I'm extremely careful to do everything by the book. No hard drugs, for instance. Yes, we allow marijuana but we exercise strict quality control. We have a reputation for sexual libertarianism but really by the standards of the outside world we are positively prudish.'

'Present company excepted.' Bognor grinned.

The swami grinned back. 'All company directors have their little perks,' he said.

'As far as money goes,' he went on, 'we are totally scrupulous. We can afford to be. We have a very great deal of it. That brewer I was mentioning, he's just one of many. We invest shrewdly, of course. And at times we may sail a little close to the wind but everything is strictly legal and above board. If anyone wishes to inspect the books he can do so whenever he likes. Even you.'

He rubbed his whiskers, and paused before continuing. 'Now the second we arrived here we had a visit from the doctor. We have our own trained medical staff here naturally but we received him kindly until it became clear that what he was trying to do was to negotiate some sort of contract for supplying illicit drugs.' The swami looked scandalised. 'As far as I could make out this was something he was already doing for others, but I didn't enquire. We sent him packing straight away.'

'Are you sure?' Bognor was startled but not totally unsurprised. Macpherson had not impressed him.

'I couldn't prove it,' said the swami, 'not in a court of law. But yes, I'm sure. The next thing was that fellow Contractor from the manor was round. Very oily he was. Now I still don't know exactly what he was after but it was to do with sex. No doubt about that. He seemed to think I was running some sort of brothel. Could people stay for the weekend. He had one or two clients who...nudge, nudge, wink, wink, know what I mean. He got quite ratty when I said we didn't go in for that sort of thing. Even got his cheque book out, which was pretty naive of him because I could buy him out twice over before breakfast.'

The swami looked more outraged by the insult to his financial strength than by the appeal to his larder of sexual goodies.

'And now Wilmslow...' said Bognor.

'And now Mr Wilmslow of the Customs and Excise,' concurred the swami, adjusting his robes, then kicking off his sandals and hoisting his legs on to the sofa. 'What a little tick he was. Dear me. Such poverty of expression too. Do you know what he said? He'd only been in here a few minutes when he looked at me − he was sitting just where you're sitting in that armchair − and he said to me, "O.K. swami, how about a slice of the action?" "Slice of the action!"' The swami repeated the words and snorted with disbelief.

'What exactly did he mean?' asked Bognor, knowing perfectly well but wishing to have it spelt out.

'What he meant, Simon dear boy, is that he and I should connive over a falsification of our Value Added Tax returns and split the profit.'

'Could he do that?'

'Easiest thing in the world.' From somewhere out in the garden a muezzin-like call disturbed the pastoral calm of morning. Seconds later it was followed by a communal mantra chant from below the window. The swami glanced at his gold Rolex. 'Excuse me just one second,' he said apologetically, and walked across to the french windows which led on to a balcony. From where he sat Bognor could see him waving beatifically back in the direction of the mantra and then dipping into his pouch for some purple papers which he scattered majestically towards the earth.

'What was all that about?' asked Bognor when he returned to the sofa and was sitting again with his legs pulled up beneath him.

'To be honest,' said Bhagwan Josht, 'I'm not entirely certain myself. My Minister for Spiritual Affairs thought it up. At noon and at six p.m. everyone has a bit of a chant and I go out and bless them. It's very popular.'

'I see,' said Bognor.

'To return to Mr Wilmslow,' said the swami, wrinkling his nose in contemplation of such a slug-like subject, 'it became quite clear in the course of our conversations that your Mr Wilmslow was doing it the entire time. Quite apart from anything else he as good as told me that he was working some sort of VAT return fiddle with everyone who was registered in Herring St George. Including, I may say, Fashions Sous-tous and that tasteless rip-off down at the Pickled Herring. That, by the way, used to be a proper pub with skittles. ' The swami sighed. 'Those two queens have ruined it.'

'You couldn't prove any of this I suppose?' Bognor expected nothing. Wilmslow was no fool, greedy though he may have been. If VAT returns had been cooked they would be cooked à point. Just so. It would take a clever investigator to identify the frauds.

'I've got a tape recording,' said the swami nonchalantly. 'Not admissible in court I don't suppose; if he were alive it would be strong enough to get him fired. It's fairly clear that he's making an improper suggestion to me.'

'And what about the others? The Contractors and Felix and Norman?'

The swami pursed his lips. 'I think you'll find he's been quite careful. Implied everything but said nothing. However if you play your cards right I should think you've got enough here to put the wind up one or two people. I'll run you off a copy before you go. Would you care for lunch?'

Bognor said, no, he'd better not. Miss Carlsbad's word-processing disk was burning a hole in his pocket and he wanted to touch base with Monica and Guy. A lot seemed to have happened that morning and the waters were growing murkier by the moment.

'I'll get one of our people to drop the tape off at the pub,' said the swami. He stood up and eased on his stout leather sandals. 'It's been super seeing you again. If ever you find the pressures of life too much you know where to come. Monica as well, of course.'

'I'm not sure I like the idea of sharing her with you,' said Bognor.

'There are ways round that,' said the swami, pausing in the passageway to tear off a strip of paper from a Telex. He frowned, then opened the door of the Communications Room and called out, 'Sister Fatimah. Sell that Hong Kong stock you bought this morning and buy Bannenbergs. And for heaven's sake go easy on gold.' A doe-eyed bride, crouched over a computer screen, glanced up and smiled.

'Right on boss, baby,' she said.

The swami smiled at Bognor. 'I like to keep things very informal except when we're actually going through some act of worship,' he said. 'I don't want them treating me as a god the entire time. That way lies certain madness.' He giggled. 'I hope you find who killed him,' he said. 'He wasn't my cup of tea, but I do draw the line at murder.'

'You think he was murdered then?' asked Bognor.

'Oh yes,' said the swami, 'beyond a peradventure.'

It was a bit of a hike back to the Pickled Herring and the sun was high in a cloudless sky. He knew he should not have worn such thick socks, let alone the grey flannel bags. He could take the tweed jacket off and swing it nonchalantly over his shoulder, but not the trousers. Nothing indecent about nobbly knees and underpants but not the done thing either. Especially when about one's government's business. One just had to sweat it out and look forward to a pint of bitter when one reached the Pickled Herring. Maybe a shower as well.

He was striding along humming Lilli Marlene and thinking wistfully of the Israeli girl paratroop clone when he heard a busy, buzzing car engine approaching briskly from behind. Yet again he was aware of the recklessness of country drivers in these treacherous high-banked lanes. He wondered if it was the district nurse who had a reputation for being the fastest thing on wheels in all the Herrings. She drove a Metro with an MG trim, and was alleged to be no better than she should be, though Bognor put this down to village gossip.

It was not the district nurse however but a scarlet Mercedes sports car with the hood down, and the driver was Samantha Contractor. She tore past him, then screeched to a halt and reversed noisily until she was alongside.

'Hi stranger!' she called, leaning across to open the passenger door and exposing large expanses of bra-less breast, 'Want a lift? You look hot.'

'I am hot,' said Bognor, guiltily remembering the photograph he had so recently picked up off Emerald Carlsbad's back path.

'Where've you been?' she asked as she crashed the gears and let out the clutch. Bognor felt himself being thrust back into the seat like he did in an aircraft just before take off. She did drive awfully fast.

'Oh, all over,' he said.

She glanced across and smiled mischievously as she let the car slide into the bend, checked the drift and accelerated away fast.

'Where's Monica?' she asked.

'Back at the Pickled Herring. She had a bad night.'

'Oh!' Sam did not seem particularly surprised. 'Come on up to the manor and tell me what you've been up to. Do you have a moment?'

Bognor looked at his watch. It was after twelve-thirty. He really ought to be getting back. On the other hand a few minutes wouldn't hurt and she was rather gorgeous. He found himself thinking back to her photo again. 'O.K.,' he said, 'just for a second.' Then before he could stop himself he found that he was blurting out: 'By the way I saw an absolutely ravishing picture of you earlier today.'

She looked across at him with interest.

'You did?'

'I was up at Miss Carlsbad's. Damian Macpherson was coming out. He dropped his file...'

Sam stamped on the accelerator again. Bognor's left hand tightened on the door handle. She was a very fast lady.

'Funny,' she said. 'I saw Damian about half an hour ago. He said he'd seen you but he didn't mention that you'd seen one of the pictures. He's good isn't he?'

They had reached the back lodge. Sam slowed for the bend, rattled over the cattle grid, then stabbed on the gas again. She seemed disturbed, thought Bognor, though he guessed she always did drive aggressively.

'How do you mean good?'

'He hasn't been taking pictures long. Perry and I have been sort of sponsoring him. He's keen to try nudes so I agreed to sit for him. If he's going to use nude models he might as well start at the top.'

'Yes.' Bognor relaxed. It was a plausible enough explanation. In any case what other explanation could there be? Sam was wonderfully sexy but also wonderfully naive. Perry was the brains. Perry might well be a crook. Sammy on the other hand was one of nature's innocents. He was sure of that. Indeed, it occurred to him suddenly that if he was going to get straight answers out of either of the Contractors it was much more likely to be from her.

They had pulled up outside the house now. A scrunching of gravel, a stench of burning rubber and life had come to a merciful halt. 'Ah!' said Sam, 'I love to live dangerously!'

'By the way,' said Bognor, trying to appear offhand and nonchalant, 'tell me about Dull Boy Productions.'

Was it his imagination, or was there a sudden slip in her composure. She was just getting out of the car and she seemed to stumble slightly. 'Shit!' she swore, slamming the door, 'I'm always snagging that wretched window handle. I'm sorry darling, I didn't catch you. What did you ask?'

'A company called Dull Boy Productions,' he repeated. 'My boss phoned about it this morning.'

'Dull Boy Productions,' she said thoughtfully, 'what a peculiar name. It doesn't mean anything to me but then Perry has so many companies. I should ask him.'

She seemed lost in thought for a moment, then looked at him almost suggestively and said, 'Darling, what about a swim? You do look terribly terribly hot.'

'I am hot,' said Bognor. 'And I'd love a swim, only I don't have any trunks.'

'Oh, if you're going to be prudish you can borrow a pair of Perry's. But no one's going to care if you swim in the buff. We usually do when we're on our own. There's no one else here. Perry won't be back for hours.'

Bognor's mouth felt dry. He wasn't sure whether he was being propositioned or not, but he did know that she was challenging him not to be a prude. He thought of her photograph and of his friend the swami and his brides and he thought, 'Dammit'. And out loud he said, 'Good idea!'

'Fine,' she said. 'You swim and I'll change into something cool and fix us a drink. I'll see you on the terrace in ten minutes.'

'Right you are,' said Bognor.

'You know where it is,' she said. Which he did, having swum there before, though always in trunks. It was a spectacularly sensible pool – half in and half out of doors. A glass screen came down to just below water level, and ran the entire width of the pool. If you wanted to move outdoors from the indoor pool you had only to duck under this window and swim on into the garden. If swimming out of doors the weather suddenly turned cold you had only to duck under the screen and swim back in. Bognor could not think why there weren't more pools like it.

He undressed in the men's changing room – they were labelled, predictably enough, Guys and Dolls – and slightly apprehensively wrapped himself in an enormous bath towel before heading out into the pool area. He did not, he had to confess, look wonderful without any clothes on, and he was not at all sure he wanted to be surprised. At least not until he was in the water. And even then... He did rather fancy Mrs Contractor and he sometimes wondered if perhaps...and some people found him quite attractive...and what in God's name would Monica say...and...

There was nobody in the pool but he wasn't taking any chances. Sitting down on the edge he did not divest himself of the bath towel until he was almost in the water, somehow managing to half sidle, half jump in with only a fleeting exposure to anyone who might be around, of what he still tended to think of as his 'private parts'. He was all in favour of others flaunting these parts wherever they wished but he wasn't sure he would ever come round to the idea himself.

It was wonderfully cool after the sticky heat of wandering around in grey flannels, and he felt pleasantly liberated. The towel was close at hand right by the steps so that if he should be surprised he could almost certainly manage an exit with decency and dignity intact. 'Aaaah,' he sighed. This was the life. If only a little more money had adhered to his fingers how much happier he would be. This was bliss. In a second he would be out on the terrace drinking champagne with the beautiful Samantha and, perhaps, who knows? He lay on his back and closed his eyes. He could lie like this for ever.

'Aaaah,' he sighed, and then suddenly changed pitch. 'Aaargh!' he gasped as he felt himself seized from below and ducked. Luckily he was in his depth but he had been taken by surprise and was gasping for air. Whoever it was had hands secure over both eyes.

'Guess who?' said Samantha, giggling. She must, he

realised, have come in from the garden without him noticing.

'Samantha,' he spluttered, 'let go.'

She giggled again. 'Not unless you promise.'

'Promise to what?' He tried to sound indignant but it had to be admitted that the proximity of her naked body was rather exciting.

She nibbled his ear. 'To kiss me passionately,' she whispered.

'Don't be ridiculous Samantha I really can't. It's broad daylight. I mean what on earth would Perry say? And Monica? Let go and don't tickle. Please, I'm not ticklish. No really I'm not. No absolutely not.'

Somehow she had managed to turn him or perhaps he had turned himself so that now her mouth was on his and her arms were enveloping him. He half opened his eyes and saw her naked breasts and nipples pressed up against his chest. 'Oh God!' he thought as she managed to force her tongue between his lips. This was awful. On the one hand it was fearfully, perhaps even dangerously, exciting. On the other it was excitingly, dangerously fearful. What was it about pain and pleasure? To his horror he realised he seemed to be returning her kiss. He tried half-heartedly to break free but she seemed stronger than him or perhaps just more determined. And he knew he was being feeble.

'Sam,' he tried to say as she relaxed her pincer grip on his mouth and gasped for air. 'Sam. This is silly. This is terribly terribly silly,' but before he could say more she had her breath back and was grinding her teeth against his and flicking her tongue around his mouth in a way that Monica would have dismissed as downright unhygienic. He had read recently that you could get AIDS from saliva and the thought galvanised him into a sudden spasm of activity. Somehow he must have got one of his feet behind her ankle because she lost her footing though not her grip and the two of them tumbled over into four foot of water. Now she did let go for a moment.

As they resurfaced Bognor was aware of a pair of very shiny black shoes more or less level with his eyes. Raising his gaze he took in pinstriped trousers, a black coat and waistcoat, black tie and white shirt, and above them a leering face, partially obscured by a 35 millimetre Canon 'sureshot' camera of exactly the kind that Monica had given him for Christmas.

'Smile please!' said the cameraman and although Bognor did nothing of the kind the camera clicked and the flash flashed. 'Terrific!' said the photographer. 'That's the end of the film. Thirty-six pictures.'

'Dandiprat!' said Bognor, ashen-faced.

'Thirty-six beautiful full colour pictures,' said Dandiprat, 'and these are wonderful little cameras. Absolutely foolproof. Never known to make a mistake. Mind you I'm a very good photographer even with more sophisticated equipment, but I thought in the circumstances...' He pressed the re-wind button, then opened the back of the camera to remove the film.

Bognor turned to Samantha.

'Samantha!' he said, 'how could you?'

For a moment she returned his stare; then suddenly looked away and flipped backwards towards the glass screen. A little shimmy of arms and legs and her preposterously appealing form was back in the garden.

Bognor did not follow. Instead he stared at Dandiprat as he felt a gentleman should stare at a peeping Tom butler who has surprised him in a swimming pool with a naked lady. Unfortunately he was only too well aware that he did not cut a very imposing figure. Dandiprat, in any case, was not looking at him but was busy extracting the yellow Kodachrome film and, when he had done so, tossing it in the air with an expression of nauseating self-satisfaction.

'Dandiprat,' said Bognor in his most officer class voice, 'I wonder if you would be so good as to pass me the bath towel at the top of the steps.'

'Certainly sir,' said Dandiprat, pocketing the film.

Bognor, slowly and deliberately waded to the stairs, and ascended them, sucking in his stomach to offset any tendency to paunch and trying to drape the towel as strategically as possible. Only when he had regained terra firma did he remember the stories of how Lyndon Johnson had humiliated his staff by dictating to them while sitting on the loo. Oppressive white South Africans were supposed to do the same sort of thing with their kaffirs. Apparently it was very upsetting for staff to have their masters' bodies paraded about in front of them; it made staff and servants feel like unpersons. Bognor therefore made a considerable show of drying himself quite naturally without any show of modesty. Unfortunately this seemed to have no effect on Dandiprat one way or another.

'Well,' Bognor realised that he could not go on drying himself for ever and that he had better take an initiative he was far from feeling, 'what have you got to say for yourself, Dandiprat?'

'With respect, sir,' said Dandiprat, 'I feel that I should be putting that question to you.'

'Now listen, Dandiprat,' said Bognor, rolling the butler's surname about in his mouth like Donald Sinden on a first night, 'since when has it been part of a butler's job to spy on his mistress and take photographs of her with her guests?'

'Compromising photographs if I might say so, sir.'

'All right, yes, they might look compromising, yes.'

'I have always regarded my most important role in life as the safeguarding of my master's interests. Sir.'

The 'sir' seemed to Bognor to be rather slow in coming. He resented this. He had always had a low opinion of Dandiprat, partly because he was so very small, partly because he was so absurdly obsequious. He had also found him unnerving because he was so bloodlessly sinister.

'It's blackmail is it, Dandiprat?' he asked. This seemed the logical conclusion. And he couldn't for the life of him see how that would help his master.

'I wouldn't put it quite like that, sir.' The butler leered.

'No,' said Bognor, 'blackmailers never do, do they?'

'I'll be brief,' said Dandiprat, suddenly assuming an air of authority which Bognor found surprising and unbecoming. 'The fact of the matter is that we're none too happy about your line of enquiry since the death of Wilmslow.'

'What do you mean "we"?' Bognor wanted to know, but the truculent butler ignored him. 'In particular,' he said, 'we don't appreciate your interest in Dull Boy Productions and I think you ought to know that if you persevere with that particular line of questioning we can't be held answerable for the consequences.' At this point Dandiprat took the film from his pocket and made a point of studying it. 'Seriously, sir,' he said, 'seems to us locals here in Herring St George that poor Mr Wilmslow was the victim of a most unfortunate accident. RIP is what we say. Nothing you can do will bring him back to life, poor bugger. And the rest of us have to knuckle down and make the best of what's left to us. Don't you think, sir?'

'Is that all you have to say, Dandiprat?' asked Bognor. The butler simpered.

'If we don't like the way you're treating us,' he said, 'then one set of these pictures goes to Mrs Bognor and one to Mr Parkinson at the Board of Trade. No wife and no job, Mr Bognor sir. And all on account of being so concerned about what happened to a poor VAT inspector who just happened to get drunk one night.'

'I have to get changed now, Dandiprat,' said Bognor. 'Do you have anything sensible to say? Or is that it?'

But Dandiprat said nothing at all. He just stood there tossing the film from one hand to the other and whistling tunelessly through his teeth.

'Melodramatic little runt,' said Bognor, half to himself, as he stomped off to change. It was a bit much. All he had done was have a swim. It was hardly his fault if he had been lying about in the pool when he was attacked by a voracious lingerie model without any clothes on. He had tried to fight her off but she had been too strong for him. He frowned. He did see that if the photographs were anything like as revealing as he imagined then they would be difficult to excuse.

'Bloody hell!' he exclaimed, getting back into his oppressively inappropriate clothes. And there was a long walk back to the Pickled Herring ahead of him. He had hoped to ride there in the Mercedes with the wind ruffling his remaining hair as he and Samantha careered down the high banked corniche into Herring St George. That was obviously out of the question now.

What was most galling was the way she had set him up. She had obviously gone straight to the wretched butler the second they had entered the house and said, Bognor of the Board of Trade is in the pool without any clothes on, I'll get undressed and you can come and take some saucy pictures of us. Which, in retrospect, was pretty upsetting. Even worse was the fact that try as he might it was difficult to feel entirely innocent.

Not that he had anticipated anything quite like that. Well...if he was absolutely honest, her suggestion of going for what used to be called a 'skinny dip' had rather excited him in a subconscious sort of way. Not that he had for an instant contemplated being unfaithful to Monica. Absolutely not. He had never been unfaithful to Monica. Not entirely anyway. Something had always conspired to prevent it happening which he always found on the one hand rather a relief and on the other immensely frustrating. Now, it seemed, he was about to incur Monica's wrath without having had the pleasure which might have made it worthwhile. There was no justice. And as for Parkinson, it did not bear thinking about. Worst of all was the idea of Parkinson handing the pictures around at lunch in the Reform Club, sucking his teeth with the Permanent Under Secretary and the Principal Private Secretary, while underneath the mimsy disapproval they would all be having a quiet giggle and a quiet salivate.

Nevertheless his mind was made up. Dandiprat and Samantha (for he had to accept that Samantha was part of a conspiracy much though it distressed him) had picked the wrong person. You couldn't blackmail a victim who refused to be blackmailed. He would go straight to Monica and straight to Parkinson and confess everything. Not that there was anything to confess. He would explain that he had simply gone for a swim when Samantha had tried to rape him.

'With no clothes on, Bognor? Is that your usual custom?' He could imagine Parkinson asking with that thin Presbyterian scepticism.

'Alone in the house with that woman and you jumped into the pool in the nude? And you expect me to believe you weren't dying for her to jump in with you?' He could visualise the quality of Monica's disbelief all too well.

Nevertheless he had no alternative. He might not broach the subject quite yet. Might just let it ride for a while and see how things panned out. Dandiprat might not need to threaten him and the films with exposure. But he didn't see how.

On his way out past the drawing room he heard a sound and poking his head around the door he found Samantha, now dressed in a white trouser suit and high-heeled gold sandals. She was pouring herself a Scotch from the drinks trolley and when she looked up at him she seemed quite distressed.

'That was a very low trick, Samantha, a very low trick indeed.'

The door opened at the far end of the room and Dandiprat slunk in, servile menace festering in every pore. Samantha looked up, then back at Bognor, and seemed on the point of words or even tears for all Bognor knew.

'And I thought you liked me,' said Bognor in a voice which was supposed to sound like ice but came out rather unimpressively strangulated. He ignored the butler, however, spun on his heel with considerable panache and exited smartly in the direction of the Pickled Herring.

SIX

Guy and Monica were waiting for him outside the pub. Or so they said. Actually they were sitting at a table on the front lawn under a parasol labelled Campari and as Bognor grumped sweatily down the lane towards them he would have said that until they spotted him they were staring into each other's eyes at close range. Monica had obviously decided Guy was not such an ass; Guy that Monica was not to be patronised. Suddenly Bognor felt less guilty about himself and Samantha in the pool.

'Hello there Simon,' called Guy. Guy was looking as cool as the younger man in the Harrods catalogue. He had the same chiselled tailor's dummy looks which Bognor, especially in his present frame of mind, couldn't abide. Same blazer too.

'Where've you been?' asked Monica. 'We were beginning to worry.' Bognor could see no evidence of concern from either party.

'You look hot,' said Guy. 'Drink?'

'I'd love a pint,' said Bognor. 'Thanks.'

Guy was on aerated water as usual. Monica asked for a glass of white wine. Her second by the look of things.

'You shouldn't be drinking,' he said, shortly. 'Remember what the doctor ordered.'

'I'm not impressed with that doctor,' said Monica. 'Nor is Guy. Guy thought he was very shifty.'

'Guy's right for once,' said Bognor. 'My information is that he's an aspiring drug pusher.'

'Where does your information come from?'

'You'll never guess. The Chosen Light himself told me.

128

Said Macpherson propositioned him as soon as he and his Blessed Followers got here. You'll never guess who he is.'

'Who?' Monica looked ungratifyingly curious.

'The swami. We were right about his being a Balliol man. But he's a real one. He sends his regards.'

Monica chewed her thumbnail. 'Too long ago,' she said, 'and there were so many flawed Indians in Balliol.'

'Bhagwan Josht,' said Bognor. 'Phoney Fred is Bhagwan Josht.'

'Is he really?' Monica smiled indulgently. 'Bhagwan Josht. He asked me to a Balliol commem one year.'

'And did you go?'

'No, I'd already promised to go with you to the Apocrypha one. It was the year you got so drunk.'

'You were drunk too.'

'So? What else did Bhagwan say?'

'Quite a bit actually. Perry Contractor came nosing around looking for some sort of sex and was sent packing. But, more interesting, he says that when Wilmslow came to check over the VAT figures he offered him a deal.'

Guy returned with the drinks.

'Did you hear that, Guy?' asked Monica. Bognor did not care for the enthusiasm in her voice. He could be quite a jealous husband.

'No.' Guy looked enquiringly at Bognor.

'I was up at the hall,' said Bognor, 'and the swami told me that Wilmslow tried to cut him in on some crooked deal to do with Value Added Tax. They'd cook up some fake figures and share the profit.'

'I was up at the hall, too,' said Guy. 'And he didn't say anything about it to me.'

'Well you were asking about alibis,' said Bognor, wiping beer froth off his lip. 'Whereas I was asking about motive. I warned you I'd have more fun.'

'I wouldn't trust that swami further than I could throw him,' said Guy. 'He was very offhand with me. Rushing off to play real tennis. Or so he said.'

'It's their holy game,' said Bognor knowledgeably. 'Did he have a good alibi?'

Guy shrugged. 'He said he was in bed with a bride of his called Blessed Orchid.'

Bognor smiled. 'I met her,' he said. 'Pretty girl. I suppose most of our potential suspects claim to have gone to bed early and stayed there all night.'

'Aha!' said Monica with a gleam. 'Tell him about your discovery, Guy.'

Bognor did not at all like this 'Listen to this Guy,' 'Tell him that, Guy' business. He decided to put any 'confession' about Samantha and the pool firmly on the back burner.

'Well it is rather interesting,' said Guy, bursting with mock modesty.

'What?' Bognor was sure it would be something irrelevant.

'The only person with a proper alibi is the padre.'

'That drunken sky pilot as Sir Nimrod would call him,' said Bognor. 'Where was he, then?'

'You're not going to believe this, old boy, but he told me he was spending the night with Lady Amanda Mandible at Groove.'

'Amanda Mandible.' Bognor frowned. 'The Society Tart.'

'Penny farthing Mandible as she's known round Annabel's,' said Guy. 'The oldest bicycle in the business.'

'I'm sorry?' Bognor was not with him.

'Sorry,' Guy flushed, 'vulgar slang I'm afraid. She has a considerable reputation as a nymphomaniac of a certain age but it's an open secret that she's also one of the top three Madams in Britain.'

'Is that so?' Bognor was not up on that sort of thing. 'Prostitution doesn't come under the Board of Trade,' he said. 'Though the Treasury seem to be taking an increasing interest.'

'No, well.' Guy was looking very self-important. 'You

can take it from me that that's who she is. So it's a very rum place for the Reverend Branwell Larch to be spending the night. Much less to be proud of spending the night.'

'Oh, I don't know,' said Bognor, 'he's probably as ignorant about her line of work as I was. You can't expect country vicars to know about that sort of thing. He's probably just a social climber. After all she does have a title of sorts. Maybe the reverend is impressed by all that.'

'There's nothing wrong with having a title,' said Monica pointedly.

'Oops! Sorry, Guy. I didn't mean to imply anything. I just meant. Oh, well never mind. What exactly are *you* implying? That the vicar of Herring St George is a sort of chaplain to a brothel?'

'I motored over to Groove,' said Guy. 'It's only ten miles away. Lady Amanda confirmed it. His name was in the visitors' book.'

'It's all very interesting,' said Bognor, 'but where exactly does it get us?'

'That remains to be seen. You see Wilmslow had been working on Lady Amanda's VAT business immediately before moving on here. As I say, she lives only a few miles away.'

'How do you know?'

'I checked with Customs and Excise as soon as I found out about Larch. I've asked them to see if there is any record anywhere of Larch having received money from Lady Amanda.'

'It's all very interesting.' Bognor tapped his pocket to make sure the computer disk was still there. 'But the only thing it actually proves is that Larch was several miles away on the night of Wilmslow's disappearance. So he can't have done it.'

'We may be looking at a conspiracy here, Simon.'

'I agree.' Bognor paused for effect. 'Tell me something,' he said, slowly, 'does the name Dull Boy Productions mean anything to you?'

Guy shook his head.

'Not offhand,' he said. 'Should it?'

'I'm not sure. But it seems to be cropping up with sudden frequency. I first heard it this morning from Parkinson, my boss at SIDBOT HQ. He said the Americans were investigating it. It's Miami based but the president is Sir Nimrod Herring and Peregrine Contractor is chief executive.'

'Sir Nimrod Herring!?' Guy and Monica combined in incredulity.

'You must be joking,' said Guy.

'Parkinson doesn't make jokes.' Bognor spoke with feeling.

'I can confirm that.' Monica spoke with almost as much feeling as her spouse.

'When Parkinson phoned this morning about Dull Boy I'm more or less certain that Felix or Norman were listening in. I cut the phone off as soon as I realised and rang back from the public call box in the village. But I think that whoever it was must have heard the message about Sir Nimrod and Dull Boy because, when I called round at Herring and Daughter, Naomi said the old boy had done a bunk rather rapidly, and just after fielding a phone call. It's only a guess but I have a hunch that one or other of the Pickled Herring boys tipped him off.'

'But tipped him off about what?' Guy was plainly exasperated at having his thunder stolen.

'Rumbled the fact that there was more to him than purveyor of gumboots and mouldy bacon to the rural proletariat,' said Monica crisply. 'He was supposed to be totally broke. That's what the VAT figures show; that's what he was saying all through his confession about Wilmslow and the blackmail business. And now it transpires he's the president of some company based in Miami. It doesn't square. Where did the money go?'

'I have a nasty feeling,' said Bognor, 'that he was only telling us half the truth. Naomi says he made a trip up to town once a month, ostensibly to have lunch with some old military muckers of his. But what if Wilmslow was blackmailing him all the time? What if old Sir Nimrod was drawing a monthly packet from his presidency of Dull Boy and passing it straight on to Wilmslow? It makes a horrid sense. You can bet your life Wilmslow would insist on cash. And nobody would trust that sort of cash in the post.'

'Pure speculation!' said Guy. 'You've got no proof at all. And what in hell is Dull Boy Productions anyway?'

'London are finding out all they can.' Bognor was pleased by Guy Rotherhithe's obvious pique. Monica looked almost impressed. He pressed home his advantage.

'After I'd been to the stores,' he said, 'I wandered off to the mysterious Emerald Carlsbad.'

Guy nodded. 'I went there. Typical dykey old trout with a raft of dogs. She claims she was at home and asleep all night. On her own though, no Blessed Orchid in sight. Though I dare say she'd have welcomed the opportunity.' He laughed sourly.

'But you didn't discover the source of her secret income, did you Guy?' He felt he was entitled to feel superior now. This made Guy's stuff about the Reverend Larch seem very small beer. At least he thought so. So, obviously, did Monica.

'Do tell,' she said. 'Is her secret as sexy as the vicar's?'

'No, not really.' Bognor allowed himself a not altogether appealing smirk. 'You'll never guess but apart from her seminal two volume treatise on *Freudian Traumdeutung in the Cook Islands* she is also the author of God knows how many pulp novels. She writes hardboiled American whodunnits as Earl J. Tuxedo; westerns as Matt Durango and, best of all, bodice-busters as Emerald A. Trawle, which as you will instantly appreciate just happens to be an anagram of Walter de la Mare.'

'She never!' said Monica. 'Good for her.'

Guy was looking frosty.

'With respect,' he said, 'that's extraordinarily interesting, but I fail to see quite how it's relevant.'

'It almost certainly isn't.' Bognor thought he was playing his cards rather effectively. Just as he conceded a point like that he trumped Guy with another. 'This, however,' and here he extracted the computer disk from his pocket, 'did seem rather more pertinent. I was in her study and on her table next to the IBM Personal she uses for her work I saw a disk labelled, would you believe, Dull Boy Productions.' He paused again.

'Get on with it,' said Monica.

'Well,' said Bognor. 'I managed to get her out of the room and slipped another disk into the second disk drive and made a copy. This is the copy.'

'The marvels of modern technology,' said Monica. 'Are you sure you pressed the right buttons?'

'We do have computers at the Board of Trade,' said Bognor. 'And I went on that course at Bracknell.' This was true. He had not been a star pupil but he had learned the basics.

'Well,' said Guy, grudgingly, 'there's no harm in putting it into one of our machines in Whelk and getting it on to a screen. But it seems rather far fetched to me.'

'Listen,' said Bognor, 'it may be far fetched but the fact that that particular company name crops up at Miss Carlsbad's, just after we've established that Peregrine Contractor is its chief executive and Sir Nimrod Herring is its president is, to put it mildly, suspicious.'

'I think it may be time we had a word with your friend Mr Contractor,' said Guy.

'He's out,' said Bognor, hurriedly. For the moment he preferred to steer clear of the manor. He didn't want Dandiprat muddying the waters with his compromising photographs. 'So was Sir Nimrod Herring when I called earlier. He's the one I want to talk to. All that long confession about Naomi's parentage and Wilmslow being a blackmailer. And never a word about Dull Boy Productions. It's very suspicious.'

'The one thing that is becoming clear,' said Monica, 'is

that the late Mr Wilmslow was a pretty bad apple. Sir Nimrod claims he was trying to blackmail him; Bhagwan Josht says he suggested fiddling the VAT returns. Sounds to me as if he got what he deserved.'

Guy Rotherhithe frowned. 'I wouldn't have said either of those two were very reliable sources,' he said. 'It seems to me just as likely that Wilmslow was a thoroughly conscientious VAT inspector doing a difficult job as well as he could. That's not an easy path to popularity. If Herring's accounts were in the unholy mess I imagine they were then of course he'd resent Wilmslow. And the swami's obviously a rogue. I don't think we should jump to too many conclusions.'

'Oh, really,' said Bognor. 'You're sounding just like Lejeune of the Yard.'

'Well maybe,' said Guy, 'but there's a lot to be said for caution and proper procedures.'

Bognor looked at his wife and winked. 'What I suggest,' he said, 'is that we have a Ploughman's Lunch or whatever anaemically pretentious equivalent they offer here. Then we can check out Herring and Daughter and then go into Whelk and ring this stuff up on the computer.'

Guy did not look especially enthusiastic but did not offer any alternative. He had a lot of waiting to do – waiting for forensic to tell him what they had discovered after cutting into the remains of Mr Wilmslow, waiting for other men to tell him if they had discovered anything at all from scouring Gallows Wood, waiting for someone to come up with a phoney alibi, waiting for someone to make a false move.

'I'm playing,' he would say to impetuous creatures like Bognor, 'a waiting game.' It was surprising how often it worked. Apparent inactivity on the part of the police frequently seemed to unnerve the criminal mind, catalysing it into unwise and unplannned activity.

So they lunched. It was a surprisingly good meal of home-baked wholemeal bread; organically grown celery and tomato; home-made chutneys and a selection of real cheeses including Single Gloucester, Colwick, Cotherstone and Cornish Yarg coated in nettles. For once they did not talk shop but gossiped instead about old times and cricket. Despite the matter in hand and the various undercurrents of attraction and hostility it was a meal the Bognors always remembered with affection. The village green was so ridiculously English; the blazing heat so ridiculously un-English. And the second pint of bitter brought on a marvellous lethargy, an almost blissful euphoria.

This feeling that everything was rosy in the garden of England was threatened at the village stores and totally destroyed at County Police Headquarters in Whelk. At the shop they found Naomi quietly loitering under the gumboots. She seemed wan and worried.

'It's not like him,' she said. 'He always tells me where he's going and when he'll be back. I mean it's different if it's just a quick trip into Whelk but he's been gone all day and not a word. And he hasn't been himself recently. Not since that bloody VAT inspector started snooping round and making a pest of himself.'

She sniffed.

'You've no idea who it was on the phone?' asked Bognor.

'Not a clue,' she said.

Guy folded his arms across the be-blazered chest and looked magisterially policemanly. He didn't fool Bognor.

'Does your father have any enemies in the village, would you say?' he asked.

Naomi Herring sniffed more noisily than before and dabbed at an eye. 'I'm not sure about him and Mr Contractor,' she said.

'You mean because Mr Contractor bought him out of the ancestral home?' said Guy.

'No, it's not that,' said Naomi. 'I don't think Daddy really liked living in the manor, not after Mummy fell in the moat. No, it was when Mr Contractor got himself elected chairman of the Conservative Association *and* chairman of the Parochial Church Council. I think Daddy could have stood one or the other but not both at the same time. And when Dandiprat took over the poppy fund I think it really was the final straw.'

'Dandiprat?!' Bognor was astonished. 'The poppy fund. You mean Dandiprat is in charge of poppies?'

'Oh, yes,' said Naomi, 'he's the village representative of the Earl Haig Memorial fund. He lays a wreath on the war memorial every Remembrance Day.'

'He never!' exclaimed Monica.

'Oh, yes,' said Naomi. 'Daddy says it's a scandal. He says Dandiprat was a conchy.'

Even Bognor who was pacifically inclined and also too young to have been conscripted was still mildly appalled at the notion of a conscientious objector in charge of the village's homage to the wartime dead.

'Dandiprat was in the pioneer corps,' said Guy. 'Never heard a shot fired in anger of course. He was cashiered too. Did time in the glass house at Shepton Mallet.'

'You've been keeping that very quiet,' said Bognor resentfully. He was uncomfortably aware that Dandiprat was beginning to seem a disturbingly villainous fellow. Not the sort that one wanted to have a hold over one. Even if one thought one could extricate oneself with a bit of fancy footwork. 'What was he in for?' he asked.

'Some sort of black market lark,' said Guy. 'Got very pally with the GIs. Cigarettes, nylon stockings and chewing gum on the one hand. Sex on the other.'

'Stockings and sex.' Monica frowned. 'That's getting a bit close to Sous-tous,' she said. 'Are you implying he's more than just a butler?'

'It was all a long time ago.' Guy shrugged. 'And he's been clean ever since. No known form.'

Naomi sighed. 'I knew I didn't like him. I do wish Daddy was back.' She sniffed.

'Yes.' Guy was embarrassed. He had a very English dislike of displayed emotion. 'We'd like him back too. There are one or two things we'd like to ask him about.'

Naomi Herring sniffed. 'I'm not stupid,' she said. 'He's in trouble isn't he?'

She looked enquiringly at the chief inspector. The chief inspector looked at Simon Bognor. Simon Bognor looked at his wife. Monica smiled at Naomi Herring.

'I'm sure there's nothing to worry about,' she said, wearing her soothing expression. 'But when he does, perhaps you could let us know at the Pickled Herring. Or call the chief inspector in Whelk and if he's not there leave a message.'

'By the way,' said Bognor, 'what sort of car does he drive? And do you have the number?'

Naomi put a hand to her forehead in a mildly dramatic manner. 'A Morris Minor. Green. RLK 887. It's rather old. But why do you ask?'

'Oh you never know.' Bognor shuffled his feet. 'If we pass an elderly Morris Minor with the number RLK 887 we'll flag him down.'

'Oh.' Naomi Herring stared at the bacon. She seemed perplexed.

Outside on the green Bognor said to Guy, 'I think you ought to put out a call to all cars. I have a nasty hunch the old boy may be in more trouble than we realise.'

'I don't like your nasty hunches,' said Guy. 'But it might be a sensible precaution. This whole place is becoming more peculiar by the minute.'

'"Ill fares the land, to hast'ning ills a prey,"' said Monica softly. 'Where wealth accumulates and men decay.'

The two men looked at her suspiciously. 'I beg your pardon,' said her husband.

'Oliver Goldsmith.' Monica frowned. 'You remember,' she said, 'surely? "The Deserted Village." Didn't you do it for "O" level?'

Bognor shook his head. '"The Nun's Priest's Tale",' he said, 'Chanticleer and all that.'

'I was only thinking,' said Monica, 'that the English

138

village has never been the same since enclosures in the seventeenth century. That's when the rot started. Villages haven't been the same since.'

'Villages have never been the same,' said Bognor sagely.

'Least of all this one,' said Guy.

Guy drove them to police HQ in Whelk. He should really have had a police driver but his title had given him Bennite notions of how to behave in order to ingratiate himself with the working class. He believed that by driving his own car he could, in some mysterious way, identify with the bobby on the beat. In matters of substance he tended to be almost depressingly orthodox along the lines laid down by his ultra-conventional old chief at the Yard. The command structure was rigidly defined and he did not tolerate insubordination. Lip service was paid to the idea that everybody should participate in discussions but it was only lip service and stiff upper lip service at that.

The car was a newish Rover, unmarked. Had he really been true to his spasmodically expressed egalitarianism he would, naturally, have driven a modest Panda car or ridden a bike. But he was only an egalitarian when it suited him. The truth of the matter was that he liked driving himself and was an appalling back-seat driver.

Monica sat in the front and held on to the door handle as they cornered occasionally on two wheels. Bognor, reclining behind, gazed at the blurred hedgerows and thought of England. No one spoke except Guy who put out an urgent call to all cars to be on the look out for Sir Nimrod's Morris. Although he said it was an urgent message he managed to suggest that the urgency was of a fairly low priority. And once the message had been delivered he lapsed into aphonia until, drawing up before the blue lamp of County Police Headquarters in Whelk, he announced, gratuitously, 'We're here.'

This was the home of the police for the recently created metropolitan county of Mid-Angleside. Mid-Angleside had previously included parts of no less than five ancient English counties but these had all been abolished and realigned in the interests of modernity, change, and progress which had been, until a year or so ago, all the rage. This mood had now changed and the clocks were going back all over Britain. Before long the metropolitan county would be abolished and the old counties reinstated leaving the great new concrete and glass metro-police headquarters as an expensive white elephant until such time as the prevailing mood changed again and it, in turn, was reinstated or, perhaps, turned over to some interesting form of 'community use'.

Guy stopped the Rover on a double yellow line just under a No Parking sign and the three entered the building. Bognor noticed and was impressed by the deference that hung in the air, not always very obviously expressed but nonetheless palpable for that.

'Come up to the office and we'll sort that tape,' said Guy taking the stairs ostentatiously two at a time as both Bognors puffed in his wake. By the time they were in his office which was large, functional and bare he was already talking into the magic box on the scrupulously neat desk top. Bognor absorbed the contrast with his own desk which invariably looked as if he was playing Pelmanism with his correspondence.

'Simon.' Guy looked across at Bognor who had plonked himself down heavily on one of the utilitarian plastic chairs. He appeared to be on the verge of clicking his fingers and Bognor was aware again of the rise in Guy's self-importance now that he was on home turf, 'Do you have that tape?'

'Tape?' Bognor frowned. 'You mean disk.'

'Tape, disk, you know what I mean. The thing you copied off Miss Carlsbad's computer.'

Bognor handed it over. Seconds later a plain girl in a Marks and Spencer dress came in and Guy said: 'Mary, take this straight down to the Computer Room and wait while Mr Jones has it printed up. It shouldn't take a second.' She smiled nervously, took the disk and hurried out.

Guy pressed some buttons on the desk. 'Dr Vernon?' he said bossily, 'Rotherhithe here. Do you have anything on Wilmslow yet? The man we found at Herring St George full of arrows.'

Dr Vernon's voice came back amplified by the box on Guy's desk. It sounded Pakistani.

'Death was due to alcoholic poisoning,' he said. 'His blood contained approximately six times the legal limit for a motorist. I would hazard a guess that he had consumed two full bottles of whisky or its equivalent.'

'Dr Vernon.' Guy sounded impatient and disbelieving. 'At what time do you think he actually died?'

'It's difficult to be certain.' Vernon's voice was distorted by the crackle of static. 'I would say between midnight and two o'clock in the morning.'

'The arrows had nothing to do with it?'

'The arrows would have killed him anyway. But they were...' here Dr Vernon gave an arid little titter '...super-fluous to requirement. One passed straight into the heart and another the neck. In my judgement either would have been sufficient to kill him. But they didn't.'

'Listen, Vernon, we know that our man was more or less stone cold sober at around nine-thirty. Could he have drunk two bottles of Scotch between then and midnight?'

'Anyone can drink two bottles of Scotch in two and a half hours,' said Vernon. 'It might kill them, it might not. Your friend Wilmslow, on the other hand, didn't drink two bottles of Scotch.'

'But you just said he did.' Guy was looking a danger-ous pink about the top of his ears.

'As a matter of fact that's not quite what I said. I said that his blood alcohol level suggested that's what he had consumed but he didn't drink it voluntarily, he was force drunk.'

'Force drunk?'

'Same as force feeding. He didn't ingest the alcohol of his own volition − it was poured down him. As far as I can make out his nose was held with something like a clothes' peg and his arms were tied. There's extensive bruising on both wrists and mouth and nose. Also it was done somewhere else. The soles of his shoes are pristine and there's a lot of damage to the undergrowth around where he was found. Not all of it was inflicted by the people who found him. My guess is that his assailants poured whisky down his throat and then carried him into Gallows Wood so that the Clout marksmen could finish him off.'

'Can you prove any of this?'

Vernon hesitated. 'It depends what you mean by proof,' he said eventually. 'In a court of law any defence lawyer would say that the deceased had evidently consumed a large quantity of whisky and wandered, insensibly, into the woods, lain down and died.'

'And the bruising?' asked Guy.

'It could be consistent with falling about in the undergrowth.'

'The clean shoes?'

'It had been very dry,' said Vernon. 'It could be argued that the shoes would not be much marked in any case.'

'But you would argue otherwise?'

'Yes I would.'

'You'll let me have your report in writing.'

'Naturally.'

'But why...' Guy drummed fingers on the desktop, 'would a near teetotaller suddenly go out and drink through two bottles of spirits?'

'That's your problem,' said Vernon. 'I'm not a psychiatrist. But if that Scotch was self-administered then I'm a virgin.'

The door suddenly opened and the plain girl in the Marks and Sparks dress put her head round it. 'There's an incoming call, sir,' she said. 'Urgent.' She was clutching a sheaf of computer paper and was looking pinker and plainer than before.

Guy held out his hand and she gave him the paper, then retreated briskly and discomfited. He began to scan it half-heartedly while dismissing Vernon with, 'Sorry Vernon, must dash. Incoming call. Let me have your report as soon as poss. I'm most grateful.' Then he flicked another switch and said, crisply, 'Rotherhithe.'

This time the flat, nasal accents of rural Mid-Angleside flooded the office. 'Sergeant Mitcham, traffic division, sir. That car, the green Morris Minor, registration number RLK 887, I'm afraid it's turned up, sir. End of a lane down Roman Bottom over towards Mailbag Corner by the junction of Watling Street and the Whelk-Nottingham road. Woman out walking her dog came across it. One occupant; elderly gentleman by the name of Nimrod Herring Bart according to his driving licence. Dead, I'm afraid. Engine running. Piece of hosepipe attached to the exhaust. Carbon monoxide poisoning.'

'Any notes?' asked Guy. As he listened he read the computer print-out his secretary had brought in. His eyes, it seemed to both Bognors, were definitely bulging.

'None that we could find, sir.'

'Any reason to suspect foul play.'

'Only that, sir.'

'What?' For a man who is being informed of the death of one of the leading characters in a murder enquiry, Chief Inspector the Earl of Rotherhithe seemed oddly abstracted.

'The fact that there were no notes, sir. The normal thing with suicides is notes.'

'They sometimes put them in the post,' said Guy, still reading the print-out. He was turning quite pink.

'Not this time,' said Bognor. 'He left in far too much of a hurry. Poor old sod. If you ask me this is fitting a pattern. Murders contrived to look like suicides.'

Guy paid no attention. 'O.K., Mitcham,' he said, 'stay at Roman Bottom until I or someone else from CID gets over. It may not look like it but this could be a serious crime.'

He flicked the switch and cut the conversation.

'That's awful,' said Monica.

'So's this,' said Guy waving the print-out at the Bognors. 'I've never read such filth in my life. If that's written by Miss Carlsbad she must have a mind like a sewer.'

Bognor focused and read out loud: 'Dull Boy Productions. Standard captions for "The Adventures of Fifi and the Dentist from Copenhagen." Or "How Mademoiselle Discovered Oral Sex". Photographs by Danish Blue pictures.'

'I say,' he said. 'Are our wires crossed?'

'My guess is not,' said Guy. Bognor read on. The text was curiously child-like in its early simplicity. 'Fifi had to go the dentist. She needed a filling.' But after a sentence or two it became quite uncompromisingly pornographic. He lapsed into silence.

'Let me see.' Monica put out a hand, but Bognor pulled away from her. 'No,' he said, 'it's not for your eyes.'

'Don't be ridiculous,' she said, crisply, 'I can take it. You forget I'm married to you. I'm practically unshockable.'

Bognor blushed. 'You might not be shocked but I'd be shocked by your reading it. It's not fit for a lady to read.'

'I'm no lady, I'm your wife.'

'That's a very silly remark. Particularly at a time like this. Two people are dead already.'

'Don't be so ridiculous. I'm a married woman of almost forty. Surely to God I'm old enough to read dirty literature.'

She snatched the paper from him and read swiftly, eyes widening as she did. 'I don't think that's physically possible,' she said after a few moments, 'even if you were double-jointed. I shall never be able to go to the dentist again. Miss Carlsbad is certainly a mistress of the double entendre. "Open wide" indeed.'

She handed the print-out back to Guy.

'Is that obscene within the meaning of the Act?' asked Bognor morosely.

'If it was published, then, yes, no question,' said Guy running a palm over sleek aristocratic hair (the sort that's dressed by Mr Trumper). 'But you can write what you want on a computer in the privacy of your own home.'

'That's not exactly keeping a private diary,' said Bognor. 'Those pornographic passages were marked Dull Boy Productions. And we know that Peregrine Contractor is chief executive and Sir Nimrod – the late Sir Nimrod – was the president. What are the connections, I want to know?'

'Whatever else, I don't see old Herring being tied up with pornography. And why would they want him anyway?'

'The usual.' Bognor smiled sardonically. 'There may have been a total collapse of all the values that we hold nearest and dearest. The fabric of feudal society may have crumbled to nothing. Village life may be only a sick pastiche of Merrie England but people are still snobs. Especially Americans. Sir Nimrod Herring Bart gave Dull Boy a touch of class and respectability. With a name like that on your masthead you could pretend to be dealing in eroticism and not porn.'

'And he did it for the money,' said Monica, 'which he needed because that rat Wilmslow was blackmailing him. I know he didn't say anything to us about Dull Boy but that stuff about him and Mrs Macpherson rang true to me.'

'Too preposterous not to.' Bognor ran his forefinger around the back of his neck under the collar as if trying to tease out some elusive or recalcitrant fragment of truth. 'So Wilmslow was blackmailing Sir Nimrod all the time. And Sir Nimrod was collecting his president's stipend from Dull Boy and passing it straight on to Wilmslow.'

'Once a month in London.' Guy was sitting with hands together as if in prayer. The tips of his fingers touched his lips which were pursed. He paused. 'Do we assume that Sir Nimrod killed Wilmslow; that he did himself in today because he couldn't live with the guilt?'

'Fat chance,' said Bognor. 'Besides, no notes. If he did kill himself he'd have told us why, especially if he had as compelling a reason as that. Also, he couldn't have killed Wilmslow on his own. Not if Wilmslow didn't walk into

Gallows Wood under his own steam. There must have been two of them if he was carried.'

'It's turning into quite a day.' Monica got up and walked to the window. She stood for a moment, arms folded across that increasingly ample – though still rather magnificent – bosom, and then turned back to face the men.

'If you ask me,' she said, 'all roads seem to be leading inexorably towards Peregrine Contractor.'

'Oh,' said Bognor, hurriedly, 'I wouldn't say that. Perry couldn't have been listening in to my phone call this morning. And that was what precipitated Sir Nimrod's hurried departure.'

'We can't be sure of that,' said Guy.

'In any case,' said Monica, 'just because he wasn't actually listening in personally doesn't mean to say he wasn't tipped off p.d.q. One of the boys at the Pickled Herring had only to get on the blower to the manor and "Bob's your uncle".'

'What have the boys at the Pickled Herring got to do with it?' asked Bognor, in a semi-rhetorical attempt at putting up a smokescreen. He had still not fathomed a way of explaining Dandiprat's photographs. 'I mean,' he continued, 'they tried to murder me with their Nouvelle Cuisine steak and then they bug the phone and cause Sir Nimrod to be tipped off. Why?'

'They tried to murder *me*.' Monica evidently felt credit was due here. She had been in the firing line. This should be acknowledged. 'And it happened after Sir Nimrod had come to us with his confession.'

'But,' – Bognor wondered if he was getting one of his amazing flashes of intuition – 'they can't have known what it was that Sir Nimrod was confessing to. They wouldn't have known about him and Mrs Macpherson and Naomi. Surely not. But they might have known about Sir Nimrod and Dull Boy Productions.'

'I don't see why,' said Guy.

'Because,' said Bognor with a logic-defying glimpse of

the obvious which would have deeply upset Parkinson and Inspector Lejeune, 'they listened to the phone call and grassed. They must have realised the significance of Dull Boy.'

'Which is more than we do,' said Monica gloomily.

'Parkinson is bound to find out more from the States.' Bognor wished he was truly confident about this. He had a feeling the 'cousins' as Parkinson now invariably called all Americans (the result of reading too many bad thrillers) would obfuscate. And Parkinson was ludicrously deferential in dealing with American intelligence agencies. They were bigger than him and his, and he allowed it to show. 'But it's obviously to do with "sex".'

'All work and no play makes Jack a dull boy,' agreed Guy. 'Even I had worked that out, Simon. But I'm not sure I see where it gets us.'

'I think it's a conspiracy,' said Bognor. 'I think they're all in it together.'

'Including Peregrine Contractor?' Guy frowned. 'I tell you, he's a bad lot, that Contractor. I know he's a friend and all that but I've had my suspicions for a long time. And,' he eyed Bognor with what looked unpleasantly like suspicion, 'that tarty wife of his is no better than she ought to be.'

'Just because she models lingerie,' said Bognor, aware that he was sounding more shrill than he meant, 'doesn't mean to say she's tarty or any worse than she should be.'

'If it's all about sex,' said Monica, 'which is, in the circumstances, a not unreasonable hypothesis, then I still don't see where the boys from the Pickled Herring come into it. Felix and Norman generate about as much sexual electricity as a limp lettuce leaf.'

'The one thing about this case,' said Bognor, 'is that we're dealing with the most deceptive appearances since those monks.'

'Friars,' said Monica. A decade ago Bognor had uncovered a spy ring using an Anglican religious community as a front. He was naive enough in those days to be surprised to find enemies of the state hiding in coarse habits. Not any more. The years had tempered him and endowed him with a scepticism which did not come naturally.

'Friars, monks, hermits, eremites, cenobites, anchorites, it's all the same,' said Bognor, sounding like Mr Toad in fullish flight. 'The point is they're none of them what they seem. Strip off a cassock and you find a Blunt or Burgess skulking about underneath. Scratch the surface of an archetypal spinster like Emerald Carlsbad and you find a Xaviera Hollander or Fiona Richmond – sisters beneath the skin, pornographers all.'

'Breastless creatures under ground I suppose,' said Monica. 'I do dislike it when you show off. Especially when you're only trying to deceive us. I said, if it's all about sex, I don't see where Felix and Norman fit into the scheme of things. Nor do you.'

'On the contrary,' Bognor's eyes flashed, 'caterers – they're caterers. Man cannot live by sex alone and so on and so forth. You've got to eat and drink. Any self-respecting Roman orgy had caterers. That was half the point.'

'You're suggesting Felix and Norman are catering for orgies?' Guy was at his most ploddishly disbelieving.

'That's exactly what I'm suggesting,' said Bognor, 'and if you don't believe me why don't you phone your friend Lady Amanda Mandible and ask her who does her food and drink?'

'It'll be Fortnums or Harrods or Justin de Blank or Lady Elizabeth Anson,' said Monica who had, from time to time, worked in the upper reaches of the catering trade and knew her gastronomic onions.

'Only if it's above board,' said Bognor. 'If it's not I'll bet you it will be Norman and Felix.'

'No proof,' said Guy. 'No proof whatever.'

'I suggest,' said Bognor, 'that we go down there and search the kitchens. Or do as I say and phone Lady Amanda.'

'I still don't see,' said Monica. 'I mean even if we accept that Dull Boy Productions is involved in some form of dubious and possibly illegal sexual activity and if we agree that the Pickled Herring does the catering for them... I mean there's no crime in it. If I provided sausage rolls for a chain of brothels it wouldn't be a crime.'

'There are sausage rolls and sausage rolls,' said Bognor darkly. 'Catering and catering.'

The three of them thought about this for a moment, then Guy stood up and said, 'I have to get down to the corpse. See that everything's done properly. No need for you to be there. I'll drop you in the village and we can get together later. I tend to agree with Monica. It all seems to be pointing in the direction of our friend Contractor but if he is the spider at the centre of the web then I think perhaps we should let him stew in his own juice for the time being.'

'Spiders don't stew in their own juice,' said Monica, 'and I'll bet Perry Contractor won't stew in his. He's too sharp for that.'

'I want a word with Norman and Felix,' said Bognor. 'If it's a question of stewing in juice they should have the answers. But while we're mixing our metaphors I think we should give Perry enough rope to hang himself. We have questions to put to both Miss Carlsbad and Felix and Norman. And after that there will be others. Time enough for Perry when we have some cast-iron confessions.'

Monica looked sceptical. 'I think he's too clever by half,' she said. By which she meant too clever for Guy and Simon and the Mid-Angleside Constabulary.

It was hazy, hot and humid by the time Guy dropped them outside the Pickled Herring. The old inn sign hung inertly, its ancient red fish flaking in the sun. Mermaid rose crowded over the porch and almost obscured the art deco of the yellow and black Automobile Association sign which, like the inn sign itself, the landlords kept meaning to remove. The AA sign would go altogether. The Pickled Herring was to be replaced with something more contemporary. Felix had hoped to commission Hockney but had failed. Instead a man called Bugle who taught at the Whelk School of Art had promised to do something clever for them.

Bognor and his wife watched as Guy's Rover climbed away from them towards Roman Bottom, Mailbag Corner and all that remained of Sir Nimrod Herring.

'Feels almost deserted,' said Bognor, as the chief inspector disappeared into the hillside.

'Yes.' Monica scuffed at the gravel. 'I wonder if we ought to go and comfort Naomi Herring? Make her a cup of tea or something.'

'Oh,' said Bognor. 'There'll be plenty of people doing that already. Ladies from the Women's Institute and district nurses. That's what villages are for. It's called good neighbourliness.'

'Ah,' said Monica, following her spouse indoors. The only sound was the gentle tick of a particularly fine George III mahogany longcase clock by James Smith of London.

'I do like that brass chapter ring and the spandrels,' said Bognor who was enthusiastic about clocks. The owners of the Pickled Herring did not have a taste which coincided with the Bognors at every point. But they did have some nice pieces. The longcase clock struck four melodically and was echoed a few seconds later by the chimes from the village church echoing out across the fields. As they faded the house seemed even more empty and quiet than before.

'I think I might take a little shufty,' said Simon. 'See if I can't find something or other incriminating.'

'Oh,' said Monica, 'I don't think you should. Snooping around doesn't suit you. It always ends in tears. It's far too hot anyway. I'm going to have a cold shower and a bit of a zizz. Why don't you?'

Bognor stared at her incredulously. 'A bit of a zizz!' he exclaimed. 'At four o'clock in the afternoon of a working day? Can you imagine what Parkinson would say? Or Guy?'

'No need for them to know,' she said. 'Not under normal circumstances. But being you I suppose you'd get caught out.'

'I don't know, Monica,' he said looking at her incredulously, 'I really don't. You sometimes amaze me, you really do.'

And he turned away, walking towards the dining room on tippytoes with cat-like tread. Monica watched him go, then shook her head, and flounced upstairs. He was the most extraordinary man, she told herself, and extraordinarily irritating at times. One of which was this.

There was no one in the dining room and so Bognor crossed it speedily and passed through the swing doors into the kitchen. It too was empty. Spotless copper pans, some very old Sabatier knives, an ice cream maker, antique wooden spoons, strings of garlic and shallots, stainless steel hobs. No people.

Bognor surveyed the emptiness for a few seconds and sighed. He had been hoping for a clue but there was nothing here. His eyes caught a cork noticeboard by a door which looked as if it might lead to a pantry. He strode across and scanned the pieces of paper. There was a butcher's bill and a list of fresh herbs and spices to order from a couple of specialist shops in London; also the Boulogne telephone number of Maître Philippe Olivier, the ubiquitous cheesemonger. He had been praying for something which might, like the Carlsbad disk, say Dull Boy Productions, but there was nothing. Nothing at all.

He sighed and scratched, aware suddenly that even in the kitchen it was devilishly hot.

Gingerly, he tried the door. It yielded but not to a pantry as he had expected but to a sort of pantry corridor which led some thirty feet to a glass back door giving on to the kitchen garden. More doors led off the corridor. The first on the left seemed very heavy, almost like the door to a safe

Bognor tried it, but it seemed very stiff. He tried again but it still wouldn't give. The third time he wrenched at it quite hard and the door opened with surprising ease so that he almost fell into the room.

Suddenly it was cold and he realised that this was the hotel cold store. A whole side of beef was suspended from a hook on the left; shelves held butter and bacon; but most surprisingly of all, stretched out on a marble slab at the far end of this gigantic fridge, was a naked woman.

Bognor gasped.

She was raven-haired and statuesque. Her skin was almost unnaturally white and her lipstick a very vivid red which matched finger and toe nails and, more surprisingly, her nipples. She looked, to Bognor, like Snow White without clothes. Or perhaps the Sleeping Beauty. Dead or sleeping? Bognor was not quite sure, though as he shivered with cold he realised that no naked person could lie like that for long even if they were SAS trained and participating in some peculiarly rigorous NATO exercise. Dead then. With a sick shiver that had nothing to do with the cold he suddenly recalled the steak last night. Surely it couldn't... tremulously he searched the lady's flanks for any sign that a pound or so of flesh might have been removed, but she was intact. No surgeon's knife had disturbed that perfect corpse.

Bognor slapped his arms against his chest. It was exceedingly chill. His breath showed foggy as a car exhaust in a December dawn. He advanced apprehensively on the body, wondering if it was anyone he knew. There was a new girl in the typing pool who, but no, she was shorter and spottier...and that girl in Dallas had a slight look except that she had a café au lait colour and this girl was all strawberries and cream. She looked odder and odder as he got closer, almost as if she had been embalmed or chiselled from some easily worked rock. Moulded in clay even. At a distance of three or four feet he paused. There was something *very* inhuman about her. He was dimly aware that some publisher or other ran a series of books of nude photographs under the generic title *Rude Food*. Publishers, it seemed to him, were increasingly interested in producing artefacts of this nature. This luscious corpse was obviously a gastronomic centrefold.

He advanced still further and ran a finger across the girl's navel. It left a faint line like the first ski on new snow. He licked his finger and frowned thoughtfully. Vanilla with a dash of Cointreau? Or was there some fruit in there too? A suspicion of mango? He reached up to a nipple and removed what looked like a glacé cherry. He was just going through the difficult process of deciding whether to replace it or eat it when he heard a sound behind him.

He spun round swiftly and saw Norman Bone and Felix Entwistle standing in the now open doorway. Norman held a meat cleaver in his right hand; Felix an open litre of tarragon vinegar. Bognor could see at once that the disabling effects of a litre of tarragon vinegar would be near total. He doubted whether Norman would use the cleaver. But it was all fairly academic. He was armed only with a glacé cherry.

'Oh, Mr Bognor,' said Felix nastily. 'Curiosity killed the cat.'

'I'm sorry,' said Bognor, 'I was just looking for some ice.'

'And instead you found Mademoiselle Fifi.' Felix grinned. 'I'd be obliged if you would put her nipple back where you found it.'

Bognor did so, wondering as he did whether there was any way he could turn the naked lady sundae into an offensive weapon. He could not think of one.

'It seems to us,' said Felix, sniffing appreciatively at the bottle of vinegar, 'that in your very particular way you are becoming as much of a menace as your late and unlamented colleague Brian Wilmslow. His problem was greed. Never satisfied, was he Norman?'

'Never,' said Norman, testing the meat cleaver. 'We

did consider cutting you in on the deal, Mr Bognor, but we decided against it. Not that you would have agreed, I suspect.'

'We formed the impression,' said Felix, 'that you were a man of integrity and therefore not to be trusted. Were we right?'

'I don't know.' Bognor was playing for time. 'It depends on the deal.'

'I doubt that.' Felix had a revoltingly obsequious smile, even more stomach-turning here than when deployed at the dining table. Bognor was beginning to realise that the 'boys' represented a tougher proposition than he had thought. 'The point is,' continued Felix, 'that your attentions are unwelcome and must cease. Alas, the only way in which we can guarantee that they cease is by ensuring that you cease also. And, by venturing in here, you provide us with the perfect opportunity.'

Bognor realised that his shivering was as much from cold as from fear.

'This is rather a remarkable room,' said Felix, smiling around it. 'As you can see it is exceedingly efficacious for storing meat and dairy produce. You wouldn't have found ice in here. There is a refrigerator next door for that. This place is just kept chill. However it does have the capacity to freeze. Freeze very hard. A few points on the dial and we can reduce the atmosphere in here to positively arctic conditions. A man would be unlikely to survive for more than a few minutes even in one of those new eiderdown overcoats. Wouldn't you agree, Norman?'

'No wind chill factor in here,' said Norman. 'And it would take a little while for the temperature to drop.'

'We could always put on the fan,' said Felix. 'But I see no reason to accelerate the process. I think we should allow Mr Bognor some minutes for quiet contemplation. I would guess that if we allow a modest reduction in temperature we could give him up to an hour of consciousness. Death should, I imagine, follow fairly soon after consciousness is lost, but we can always check with Doc Macpherson about that. One of us can make the sad discovery around about six o'clock.'

'That's murder,' said Bognor.

'But extremely difficult to prove,' said Felix, 'just as it's extremely difficult to prove that Wilmslow was murdered. Or poor Sir Nimrod. Poor Sir Nimrod.'

'Sir Nimrod was murdered?' Still Bognor was playing for time, though he could see no way out of this predicament. Even with less than an hour to live, his professional curiosity did not desert him.

Norman looked at Felix. Felix looked at Norman. They smiled with a wan mock compassion.

'Poor Sir Nimrod,' said Felix. 'His nerve was failing. He had to go.'

'Tell me one thing,' said Bognor, mind desperately trying to find a way of stalling, 'I mean, what exactly *is* Dull Boy Productions?'

The 'boys' looked at each other and smiled again. Not very pleasingly.

'In view of your imminent demise,' said Felix, 'we can perhaps tell you a little something though really we know remarkably little. We have been to one or two of their little soirées but...well let's just say that they're not entirely to our taste. We're only humble caterers.'

'Fiddling your VAT returns and constructing obscene confections for orgies.'

'It's all quite harmless,' said Felix. 'We do have a little stake in the company, but it's very little. And it's true the books wouldn't stand up to a very detailed examination although Brian Wilmslow was ever so clever. Cooked them quite beautifully. We shall miss him.'

'Erotic cuisine is a very considerable challenge,' said Norman. 'I spent days on Fifi. We've come a long way since it was just naked ladies leaping out of cakes. You've no idea of the sophistication. The things you can do with meringue!'

'It all sounds perfectly revolting,' said Bognor. 'And I don't understand why you bothered. You've got a perfectly decent business here.'

'Brian Wilmslow was very persuasive,' said Felix. 'And there's a lot of money in it. Also there's ever such a nice sense of community involved. Almost everyone in the village is a Dull Boy or a Dull Girl one way and another. All except for that dreadful bogus swami and his harem. It's a real co-operative.'

'It can't be a real co-operative,' said Bognor. 'There must be a Mr Big. Someone must run it. Peregrine Contractor I suppose.'

'Now that *would* be telling,' said Felix. He giggled softly. 'Good night Mr Bognor. Nice knowing you. And don't worry about the bill. We'll make that our little gift of condolence for Mrs Bognor. A token of our respect.'

And very suddenly they stepped outside. Bognor heard a key turn in the lock and footsteps walk away down the flagstones. Then it was silent, and already it was bitterly cold.

Bognor started to jump up and down.

Monica had second thoughts about her shower and her zizz as soon as she got upstairs to Myrtle. It was the thought of the bereaved and destitute Naomi Herring all alone among her gumboots and bacon which was preying on her conscience. It might be that the good samaritans of Herring St George would converge on the stores bearing tea and sympathy, but Monica had formed a low opinion of the good neighbourliness of this particular village. She suspected that there would be precious few shoulders for the squire's daughter to cry on.

She was almost right.

On entering the stores she found that Miss Herring was almost alone but not quite. The professionals, in the person of God's representative in Herring St George, had arrived. The Reverend Branwell Larch had come to dispense his own particular brand of extreme unction – and extremely unctuous it was.

'"The Lord God giveth and the Lord God taketh away",' he was saying when Monica arrived, '"and in the midst of life we are in death. Just as in the midst of death we are in life."'

Monica felt like saying 'Right on, Brother Larch'. But instead she said, 'Good afternoon, Naomi. Good afternoon Mr Larch.'

'Good afternoon, Mrs Bognor!' said Mr Larch. 'It is Mrs Bognor, isn't it? This is a sad day, a sad day indeed. "And God shall wipe away all tears from their eyes; and there shall be no more death, neither sorrow, nor crying, neither shall there be any more pain."'

Monica treated him to a shrivelling glare. 'For the former things are passed away,' she said, tartly.

'"And he that sat upon the throne..."' began the clergyman, whose breath smelt of double strength mints and alcohol of dubious origin. He did not continue the quotation because he was stopped in his tracks by the second barrel of Monica's disdainful stare. Monica knew Revelation backwards.

'I am sorry,' she said to Naomi, 'he seemed such a nice man. I'm afraid my husband and I are partly to blame. I mean if we hadn't started investigating Mr Wilmslow's death then perhaps...'

'It's not your fault,' said Naomi. 'It was all going wrong even before they killed that horrible man.'

'What happened to Mr Wilmslow was an accident Naomi, my dear,' said Larch, sharply. 'An accident...just as your poor dear father's death...well, by his own hand did he perish and by his own petard was he hoist.'

'Oh, shut up!' said Monica.

The clergyman had a complexion green as the grey Limpopo. Greasy as the Limpopo too. It turned greyer and greasier yet and acquired an additional livid pink, suggestive of tropical sunset. His lip quivered and a small, creamy bubble of spittle appeared at the left hand corner of his mouth. Not a pretty sight.

'The Lord is not to be slighted thus,' he said.

Monica could look amazingly fierce. '"Beware of the scribes,"' she said, '"which love to go in long clothing, and love salutations in the marketplaces, and the chief seats in the synagogues, and the uppermost rooms at feasts: Which devour widows' houses, and for a pretence make long prayers."'

Mr Larch gaped, jaw dangerously adrift.

'Before long,' said Monica, taking advantage of her advantage, 'my husband and I and Chief Inspector the Earl of Rotherhithe will want to know why a man of the cloth is consorting with the likes of Lady Amanda Mandible. And talking in a very bad pastiche of the language of the Authorised Version. "The Lord is not to be slighted thus" indeed. Is that something you made up or is it the alternative form of community worship as practised by the Bishop of Durham? Better men than you have been unfrocked, Mr Larch.'

This little tirade had very much the effect intended. Monica had correctly judged the reverend gentleman to be more mouse than man as well as very small fry in the Dull Boy conspiracy. If indeed he was involved in it at all. Or if, come to that, there *was* a Dull Boy conspiracy. The words 'guilty not proven' kept reverberating around her grey matter.

'If you were a man, Mrs Bognor,' said Mr Larch, 'you'd be hearing from my solicitors.' He contorted his features into the ingratiating clerical apology for a smile made popular by the Reverend Obadiah Slope and said to Naomi Herring, 'If there is anything ...anything at all...that I can do to help, then you have only to ask. I shall remember you in my prayers.' Then he retrieved his theatrically brimmed black hat from beside the bacon on the counter, hitched up his cassock and scuttled away.

'Not a very nice sort of person,' said Monica.

'I think he meant well,' said Naomi. 'It's just his manner.'

'His manner is very unfortunate,' agreed Monica, 'and he has the filthiest finger nails. I shouldn't like taking communion from him.'

'No.' Naomi took a handkerchief from the folds of her smock and blew her nose very noisily. The handkerchief was very used and dirty and, Monica realised too late, her fingernails were also chipped and stained. 'Thank you for coming, Mrs Bognor,' she said, when she had finished her trumpeting. 'It's awfully thoughtful of you. I don't think it's really sunk in yet.' She smiled tearfully. 'I know he didn't do it,' she said. 'I'm sure of it. No matter how bad things got there's no way he would ever have killed himself. He wasn't that sort of person. And also he left a message.' She dabbed at her eyes with her dirty rag. 'I didn't tell you before because it...well because I didn't know then even though I had a nasty feeling...you know how you always have feelings about people you're very close to and it wasn't until I knew for certain that he was dead that, oh dear...' She started to snuffle again and was unable to talk for a few moments. Monica put an arm round her and made consoling noises.

'The message,' said Monica, when she judged the bereaved woman had had time to compose herself. 'What exactly was the message?'

'It was rather peculiar,' said Naomi, 'like a crossword clue. He was awfully good at the crossword. He said to tell your husband that if anything happened he must look for a bad penny ha'penny.'

'Are you sure?' Monica was startled. 'A bad penny maybe. Or a penny farthing. But a penny ha'penny I don't understand. Why did he have to be so cryptic?'

'I've been thinking about that,' said Naomi. 'And the only answer that makes sense is that he didn't want me to know.'

'What do you mean?'

Naomi hesitated. 'Well,' she said, 'it may seem silly but he was always frightfully protective towards me. Only child and all that, I suppose.' Her mouth started to wobble and her voice to quaver.

'Yes,' said Monica, encouragingly.

Naomi made an effort to pull herself together. 'So if there was someone who was, you know, bad, someone who was a threat, then he wouldn't want me to know who it was.'

Monica looked at her with new respect. It sounded like a reasonable piece of analysis. Sir Nimrod would not have liked his daughter to become embroiled in the Dull Boy Productions mess if he could possibly avoid it. And yet he had obviously been anticipating trouble. Trouble bad enough to leave messages about. Unfortunately although the clue was cryptic enough to elude Naomi (which was what he had presumably intended) it was also too cryptic for Monica. And if it was too cryptic for her it would assuredly be too cryptic for her beloved husband let alone for Guy with his meticulous, methodical, boring ratiocinatory approach.

Out loud she said, 'I wonder what it means. You've no ideas?'

'None.' Naomi started to snivel again.

'He didn't collect old coins for instance?'

'No.'

'Well.' Monica grimaced. 'I shall pass it on to my husband and we'll just have to hope that someone or other will be able to come up with an answer.' She smiled at the forlorn Naomi Herring, miserably aware that she was no more help to her than the ghastly vicar. 'If I were you I'd have a very stiff drink and a good cry. And if you want to come and cry on someone's shoulder just nip over to the Pickled Herring and have a good cry on mine.'

Naomi sniffed and smiled wanly and said she was very grateful and yes she might open the bottle of port Sir Nimrod had won in a raffle at Easter and she might just come over later for a bit of company. Monica felt that after all she might have been of a little solace.

Bognor was not in their room when Monica returned. It was half an hour since he had set off on his snoop. This on its own might have been mildly worrying but what really threw her was that she had passed Felix Entwistle and hadn't liked the way he smiled at her. She seldom liked the way men smiled at her but this particular smile had been qualitatively different. Greasier if possible than the Reverend Larch's reptilian bared dentures. The smile of someone who knew something unpleasant which put him at an advantage and which he was not going to divulge until later. A smile which suggested, didn't it, that something nasty had happened to her husband. 'Oh, come on, Monica!' she said to herself, out loud. 'Don't beat about the bush. Felix and/or Norman have done something horrid to Simon.'

The question was what should she do about it.

She could, she supposed, go on a snoop herself. But since Felix and Norman were evidently back home there was no way she could snoop undetected. She could confront them: 'Oh, Norman, Oh, Felix. Have you seen my husband, he was having a bit of a snoop round your kitchen and office and he hasn't come back?' Another no-no. She could imagine the leering response.

Reluctantly she realised that she needed assistance. Normally her support came from her husband. He, obviously, was unavailable, which meant, in present circumstances, that she should turn to Chief Inspector the Earl of Rotherhithe. She reached out for the phone, then remembered, just in time, that it was a dangerous instrument. She would have to walk over to the phone box on the green.

She was halfway across the sward and closing in on the little red sentry box which was Herring St George's main link with the outside world when she saw an emerald green Bugatti steaming down the hill escorted by saffron-clad outriders on Harley Davidson motorbikes. The little cavalcade zoned in on her and closed before she could reach the phone. The second the Bugatti stopped the driver pushed his World War Two flying goggles back on his forehead and beamed a toothy greeting.

'Monica,' he exclaimed. 'Long time no see.'

'Good heavens!' she said. 'Bhagwan Josht!'

'Not any longer,' laughed the swami. 'I am by way of being a living god, as Simon will have told you. A fitting career for a Balliol man. But where is he? I feel he is in great danger.'

'How do you know? Has your divinity given you ESP?'

'In a manner of speaking, yes. A combination of intuition and Citizens' Band radio. The natives around here are not exactly friendly, Monica, and we therefore make it our practice to listen in to police messages on their wavelength. It is as well to be prepared for any unpleasantness.'

'So what have you heard on the radio?'

'That Sir Nimrod Herring has been murdered and that Simon is pursuing investigations in the village. I'm no policeman but it seems to me that whoever is running this Dull Boy Productions caper has started to panic. As I understand it your friend the chief inspector is detained at his office in Whelk which means that Simon is walking around unprotected and at the mercy of some homicidal maniac.'

Monica gazed incredulously at the four young men in combat fatigues astride the silver Harley Davidsons. Then at the exquisite white robed oriental girl in the Bugatti passenger seat. 'So you're giving him a bodyguard?' she said.

The swami laughed. 'I thought it best if you moved out of the pub and stayed up at my place until the murderer is apprehended. Which can't be long if he goes on like this. I'll wait while you pack.'

'But Bhagwan,' said Monica, 'we can't do that. I don't even know where Simon is. He's vanished.'

'Vanished?!' The swami's eyebrows shot up. 'Great Scot!' he said. 'Where did he vanish? And how?'

'He went off on a snoop,' said Monica. 'He thought the coast was clear and there was no one around so he decided to case the Pickled Herring. He's very suspicious of Felix and Norman.'

'He is entirely correct to be suspicious of Felix and Norman,' said the swami. 'They are absolutely not to be trusted. In my view they are two very dangerous men. Is Simon armed?'

'I very much doubt it.'

'Then there is not a moment to lose. Squeeze in!'

Monica got into the Bugatti which was, as the swami implied, a very tight fit, and they drove the fifty or so yards to the Pickled Herring very fast.

'You two go round the back,' ordered the swami. 'The rest stay with me.'

As they entered the hall, Felix appeared, shooting his cuffs, and smiling nervously.

'Yes,' he said, ingratiatingly.

'I'm looking for my husband,' said Monica. 'He's gone missing.'

Felix frowned, put a hand under his beautiful blazer and massaged his chest thoughtfully. 'I'm sorry to hear that Mrs Bognor,' he said. 'How can I help?'

'I thought,' said Monica, 'you might have seen him.'

'I'm afraid not.' Felix shook his head and managed to look genuinely regretful. 'He's probably just gone for a walk. It's a lovely afternoon, though I shouldn't be surprised if we don't have a bit of a storm later on. Getting a bit close.'

'Leave this to me, Monica,' said the swami. He advanced to within inches of Felix so that had he not been at least six inches shorter his nose would have touched the hotelier's. 'Now listen, Entwistle, Mr Bognor is a very old friend of mine, and if anything has happened to him you're going to be sorry. And if you won't tell me where he is my men and I are just going to have to search the place. We may make a mess. So are you going to tell me?'

'You've no right,' said Felix. 'I shall call the police. You can't just barge in here.'

'I just have,' said the swami, and he pushed past the

unhappy Felix, who, intimidated by the impressively con-
structed bodyguards, made no effort to stop him.

In the kitchen they found the two other guards in noisy
conversation with Norman. Like his partner, Norman was
expressing affronted indignation, invaded privacy and
general umbrage, but in a manner which was not altogether
convincing.

'There's a locked door out the back,' said one of the
guards, a six-foot-three negro with LOVE stencilled across
his uniform, 'and chef won't open it.'

'Chef had better do as we ask,' said the swami, 'or we'll
break his door down.'

'This is a disgrace!' said Norman. 'It's a fridge. If you
open it before six o'clock an extremely elaborate mousse
full of incredibly expensive ingredients will be totally
ruined. Ruined.' He seemed genuinely distressed.

'There are a couple of crowbars in the boot of the
Bugatti,' said the swami improbably, 'so it shouldn't take
a second.'

Felix looked at Norman. Norman looked at Felix. Felix
shrugged. Norman shrugged.

'Bang goes the mousse,' said Felix.

'*C'est la vie*,' said Norman. He reached in his pocket and
pulled out a bunch of keys, selected one and handed it to
the swami. Together they all moved outside to the fridge
door, which opened easily enough to emit a blast of freezing
fog.

'Jumping Jehoshaphat!' the swami recoiled for a second.
'It's Simon and a naked woman. Quick men! Get them out!
Simon's alive, I think, but the girl looks as if she's frozen
to death.'

'Don't touch Fifi,' shouted Felix. 'She's a mousse.'

The guards realised this almost as soon as they tried to
move her, but it was obvious – just – that Simon was flesh
and blood. He was lying on the floor vainly attempting to
do what appeared to be a press-up. The two biggest guards
grabbed him under the armpits and hauled him out. He

was not an encouraging sight. There was practically no colour in his cheeks and his eyebrows had turned a frozen white as well as growing much larger than usual – a sort of icicle effect. His clothes were quite stiff and covered in fine white powder like snow and a small greenish icicle protruded from one nostril. Not pretty.

'Abominable snowman!' exclaimed the swami, shocked, but relieved to detect signs of life. 'We must thaw him out but not too fast.'

'How about my hair dryer?' asked Monica and was on the point of fetching it from Myrtle but the swami said it would be too much of a shock to the system. It was like bringing a diver up from the deep. Slowly, slowly. If you went too fast he'd get the bends. Same with Bognor. Too violent a change from cold to hot might bring on a coronary.

It was rather like watching one of those Richard Attenborough television films about life in the jungle or under the Pacific. With clever and patient photography you could actually show flowers growing or alligators being hatched. They sat Bognor on a stool and loosened his collar and tie and the swami slapped him once or twice, quite gently, on the cheeks. Even as they watched Bognor went from translucent blue to white and then pink. Like a human traffic light. His eyebrows melted and dripped down his front and his mouth opened. Words emerged.

'Christ, it's hot!' he said. 'Water.'

Monica ran a glass from the tap. Local spring water. No fluoride or other additives.

Bognor drank, deeply, gasping, then held out the empty glass.

'I think I could use another of those,' he said. 'I dreamed I was Captain Oates or Scott of the Antarctic. Had I lived I should have had a tale to tell of the hardihood, endurance and courage of my companions which would have stirred the heart of every Englishman. These rough notes and our dead bodies must tell the tale.'

'Oh, shut up!' said Monica, returning with more water which he drank noisily. He was obviously recovering fast. 'What happened?' she asked.

Bognor scratched his head. 'Happened?' he said reflectively. 'Well, I went into this sort of fridge thing and there was a dead girl lying on a slab only when I pinched her nipple it came away in my hand. It was a glacé cherry and she was some sort of pudding. Vanilla, I think.'

'One of them said her name was Fifi,' said the swami. 'By the way, where are Entwistle and Bone?'

Felix and Norman were nowhere to be seen.

'Don't worry,' said Monica, 'they can't have got far. If anywhere. What happened after you pinched Fifi's nipple?'

'Felix and Norman came in,' said Bognor, 'armed with a hatchet and a bottle of vinegar. They said they were going to lock me in and turn down the heating if you see what I mean. Freeze me to death. It would have looked like an accident.'

'Like all the other murders,' said Monica, 'except you were saying, Bhagwan, that Sir Nimrod definitely didn't commit suicide. How did they know?'

'There was a bruise,' said the swami, 'under his hair, above the right ear. He'd been knocked unconscious. Then the murderer fixed up the tubing to the exhaust pipe, left the engine running and did a bunk. Not difficult.'

'How are you feeling, darling?' Monica could be solicitous on occasion. And she was fond of the old thing, especially when he seemed on the verge of departure. 'Another five minutes and you'd have been a goner,' she said.

'Bit wobbly.' Bognor tried a smile which only half succeeded. 'I think it's time Guy started arresting people,' he said. 'After all, Norman and Felix have had two goes at attempted murder already.'

'Difficult to prove,' said the swami.

'But they locked me in their fridge,' protested Bognor.

'They'd say it was an accident,' said the swami. 'Their word against yours. And what, a jury would want to know, were you doing in their fridge anyway?'

'Investigating,' said Bognor. 'For God's sake, I am a bloody Board of Trade investigator. Any jury worth their salt would realise I have to spend a lot of time in other people's fridges. It's that sort of job.'

The swami looked at Monica and both raised eyebrows.

'I wouldn't rate your chances, Simon,' said the swami, 'and in any case I don't think Norman and Felix are more than quite small fry. They're involved in this but they're not big enough to be bosses. They're little men.'

'I see,' said Bognor.

'Oh, I almost forgot,' said Monica, 'Sir Nimrod left a clue with Naomi before he left. Said that if anything happened to him we were to blame it on a penny ha'penny.'

Bognor stared blankly at his spouse.

'I think I ought to have a smidgeon of alcohol,' he said. 'I mean what sort of a clue is that for goodness sake?'

'We think,' said Monica, patiently, 'Naomi and I, that he made it cryptic because he didn't want Naomi to know who he meant. It could have been dangerous for her and he didn't want her to be involved. But he assumed that a special investigator would know at once what the clue meant.'

'There's no need to be rude.'

'I'm not.'

'Yes, you are. You're implying that I'm too stupid to crack the code.'

'I'm not,' protested Mrs Bognor, 'but you can't crack it, can you?'

'Not at the moment. But you seem to forget that I have only this minute returned from the valley of the shadow of death. I shall solve it in due course when I've done some more thawing out and had a drink or two. Where is Guy?'

'Whelk,' said Monica.

'I suppose we ought to have a chat to him.'

'I suppose so.'

'I think,' said the swami, 'that the first thing is that you should both come to Herring Hall at once. You can discuss it all there and phone Guy. I don't think this is a good place to stay.'

'More intuitions?' asked Monica.

'Perhaps,' said the swami, smiling.

SEVEN

Bognor made two telephone calls as soon as they had reached the safety of Herring Hall.

The first was to Guy. Guy sounded weary and none too impressed by what Bognor had to tell him.

'It's not an offence to make mousses in the shape of naked ladies,' he said, 'the so-called clue is hopelessly inconclusive, not to say incoherent. The Herring girl probably invented it. She struck me as being very simple if not actually having a few screws loose.'

'But they tried to freeze me to death.'

'It could have been a mistake.'

'You don't think that, surely. I'm telling you they deliberately locked me in there and turned down the thermostat.'

'I think you've been overdoing it Simon. Maybe you should take a break. Food poisoning and freezing all within twenty-four hours. That sort of experience imposes severe strains. I think you should go back to London and leave it to me.'

'Leave it to the professionals, you mean.'

'I didn't say that.'

'You implied it.'

'I'm sorry if you got that impression.'

'In any case,' Bognor was most put out, 'I can't go back to London. I'm under orders.'

'We can soon change that.' Guy sounded unnecessarily menacing.

'I'm staying on this case,' said Bognor, 'if it's the last thing I do.'

'At the present rate of progress it almost certainly will

be. They've tried to do you in twice. Maybe it's going to be third time lucky.'

'There's no need to be like that.'

'I'm sorry.' Guy suddenly sounded as weary as Bognor felt. 'It's been a hard day. I suggest you and Monica get a good night's sleep. We'll talk in the morning.'

The conversation with Parkinson was more satisfactory in content if not in tone. Conversations between Parkinson and Bognor were always brittle. That was the nature of their relationship.

Before he could phrase his initial question Parkinson had got in first.

'And where, pray, have you been disporting yourself, Bognor?' enquired his boss, beadily. 'I made enquiries at Mid-Angleside Police in Whelk and also at that ludicrously named hotel. Neither seemed to know where you were. I even rang your friends the Contractors but the only person there was the butler who was quite uncivil when I mentioned your name.'

'Dandiprat.'

'I beg your pardon.' Parkinson sounded quite affronted. 'What exactly has numismatics to do with it?'

'Numismatics?' Bognor did not recall having said anything about numismatics.

'You said "Dandiprat",' said Parkinson irritably.

'It's the name of the Contractors' butler,' said Bognor equally irritably. 'But that is by the by. I have moved from that ludicrously named hotel because the proprietors first attempted to poison me and then, this afternoon, tried to freeze me to death. So I'm moved up to the swami's ashram at Herring Hall.'

There was a prolonged silence from the other end of the line.

'Blast!' said Bognor, 'we've been cut off. God knows what the old fool was blathering on about. He seemed to think I said "numismatics" when I said "Dandiprat". He really is showing his age.'

'The old fool is still here, Bognor,' said Parkinson more irritably than ever. 'I was indulging in what might best be described as a "stunned" silence. First poison, then freezing and now you're in an ashram in the middle of the English countryside.'

'Yessir.'

'All in a day's work, eh, Bognor?'

'Well, as a matter of fact, it has been, yes.'

'Is there anything else you'd like to tell me?'

'Sir Nimrod Herring has been killed.'

'The president of Dull Boy Productions?'

'Yes.'

'Why wasn't I told of this?'

'You were. I mean you are. I'm telling you now.'

Bognor could visualise the grinding of teeth that must be taking place. Perhaps Parkinson was even snapping a pencil or two in half. His blood pressure must be a worry.

'How was Sir Nimrod killed?'

Bognor told him.

'And what do you imagine was the motive for this?'

Bognor took a breath. 'Just after your phone call this morning Sir Nimrod left home in rather a hurry. According to his daughter, Naomi, he seemed very agitated, but he didn't say where he was going. My guess is that Entwistle and Bone at the Pickled Herring overheard you saying that we knew that Sir Nimrod was president of Dull Boy and passed on some message to the old boy.'

'Why would they do that?'

'Either to warn him that we were on his trail or – which looks more likely – to nobble him before he could spill any more beans. He'd spilled enough the night before.'

'Hmmmm.' Bognor could only hear the hum of Parkinson's voice but he could picture the contemplative peer at the portrait of Her Majesty the Queen, the impatient drumming of fingertips on the top of the regulation civil service desk. The boss at bay.

'Well, Bognor,' he said eventually, 'our cousins on the

other side of the big pond have sent us a wee bit more information on the subject of Dull Boy Productions. It appears to have something to do with the late President Kennedy: All work and no play...'

'...makes Jack a dull boy,' said Bognor, involuntarily. 'It hadn't occurred to me that Jack was *that* Jack.'

'Bear with me a moment please, Bognor.' A note of depressing weariness had crept into Parkinson's voice. 'As you may be aware, it is quite common knowledge that the late President Kennedy was in the habit of curing his migraines with women, if you follow me. Or so it is alleged.'

'They do say sex is a wonderful panacea for almost everything,' said Bognor, 'although Monica and I...'

'Please spare me your revelations, Bognor.' Parkinson sounded even more deflated than before. 'I don't think I could stand the excitement.'

'Sorry,' said Bognor.

'I'm not suggesting that the late president was in any way involved in Dull Boy Productions, I'm merely giving you background information. That is how the company got its name. It's the derivation.'

'I see,' said Bognor. 'But derivation apart, what exactly does Dull Boy do?'

There was a rather pregnant pause. Parkinson was not especially prudish in public at least not by civil service standards but he was obviously finding this embarrassing. 'As far as I have been able to ascertain from our cousins,' he said, 'the company began as a cheap tour operator offering packages to Manila and Bangkok. You'll see what I'm getting at.'

'Massage parlours,' said Bognor.

'Precisely,' agreed Parkinson. 'The enterprise appears to have been controlled by the Mob or the Organisation or the Mafia or whatever we're supposed to call them these days. It was very tatty stuff frankly. Very tatty. Our cousins began to get very concerned about some of the diseases which these tourists were picking up and importing into the States.'

'AIDS,' said Bognor.

'Things like that. Anyway for whatever reason the people who control Dull Boy decided, in the jargon of the market place, to "diversify" and "go upmarket". For the last few years they have been organising the same sort of tours to this country.'

'You mean "stately home sex", and "titled ladies for sale"?'

Parkinson sighed disapprovingly. 'I was rather afraid you'd understand the idea altogether too quickly,' he said. 'The man I spoke to at Langley quoted some passages from the Dull Boy brochure. Frequent references to Eton, the Brigade of Guards and even, I regret to say, the Royal Family. It's extremely distasteful. HMG is concerned at the highest possible level. And I mean highest. I'm not just talking about the British Tourist Authority.'

'And this whole operation was being presided over by Sir Nimrod Herring?'

'He was a front obviously. Gave the thing respectability. We're talking about a lot of money here, Bognor. Dull Boy's clients are chief executives of some of the world's biggest corporations. They require absolute discretion, exclusivity and above all what they call "prestigiousness".'

'And they're still old fashioned enough to think that an oddly named English baronet guarantees all that?'

'In my experience, Bognor, a great many of our American cousins are profoundly old fashioned particularly where the British are concerned. They regard us purely as a source of entertainment and in that sense they think of us as being pickled permanently in the 1920s. I regret to say that even the more sophisticated of our colleagues in the intelligence world take that view. It even extends to their estimate of the Special Investigations Department of the Board of Trade.'

Bognor was tempted to make a facetious remark but thought better of it. Instead he said, 'And the headquarters of this dubious organisation is here in Herring St George.'

'It's registered in Miami as I said this morning. But all the evidence points to the real centre being Herring St George,' agreed Parkinson.

'A sort of cottage industry,' said Bognor.

'You could put it like that. Obviously Wilmslow was getting too close for their comfort and so he was eliminated. Equally obviously Sir Nimrod was on the verge of turning Queen's evidence and had to be shut up.'

Bognor wondered whether now was the time to voice his suspicions about Wilmslow being an over-greedy accomplice rather than a successful sleuth. He decided not to. Parkinson had had enough shocks for one day, and the revelation was no longer particularly relevant.

'And the Americans insist that the boss of all this is Peregrine Contractor?'

'His is the name on the masthead,' said Parkinson, not unreasonably.

'Could be a front like Sir Nimrod Herring.' Bognor had a soft spot for Perry Contractor. If things were leading where they seemed to be leading his friend was about to go down with a life sentence. Bognor didn't want that.

'There's no reason,' said Parkinson. 'A name like that doesn't suggest anything much one way or another. If his name is on the masthead it's because he's what it says he is. There is one thing that's slightly bothering the Yanks though. Apparently in the old days of the cut price tours to the Far East the boss was a man called Manuel Henrici. A very nasty piece of work indeed. Shortly before Contractor took over Henrici vanished. A few weeks later the police got a tip-off and were pointed towards a swamp just north of Miami. They found a body. Or remains of a body. Seems the alligators had got there first. No way of identifying him for certain.'

'Dental records?'

'When I say body, Bognor, I mean body. Perhaps torso would be more accurate. Evidently he had a naked lady tattooed on his right buttock. There were traces of that but they were regarded as inconclusive. Anybody might have such a tattoo. In parts of Florida I understand they're positively commonplace.'

'And if they were trying to make it look as if it was this man, Henrici the Mob could have got hold of any old corpse and stuck a tattoo on its bottom.'

'The thought did cross a number of minds,' said Parkinson. 'Not least because this Henrici had done a vanishing trick once before, years back in Truth or Consequences, New Mexico. He'd been called Jimmy Montano and he was wanted for a bank robbery. Next thing anyone knew he was a mobster in Miami, specialising in vice and narcotics.'

'So some people think he could still be the mastermind behind Dull Boy?'

'It's regarded in some quarters as being conceivable,' said Parkinson. 'However, as you should know by now I'm not much of a one for melodrama and conspiracy. My guess is that the body in the swamp belonged to Jimmy Montano, alias Manuel Henrici.'

'I see,' said Bognor. 'So the Americans expect us to arrest Peregrine Contractor?'

'In the past they've found it impossible to nail Dull Boy down. Partly because they're operating over here, and partly because of the influential names involved. Another problem is that a lot of the girls are enthusiastic amateurs recruited by some high class Madam called Lady Amanda Mandible. At least that's the story. Now that there's the possibility of a murder charge the cousins are very excited.'

'Does Guy Rotherhithe know all this?'

'I understand he's being informed even as we speak.'

'Oh.' Bognor pondered. 'What do you want me to do?' he asked.

'Stay out of trouble,' said Parkinson. 'And report back here when Chief Inspector Rotherhithe has cleared it all up.'

'Yes,' said Bognor. He felt properly snubbed, as he so

often did after talking to Parkinson. However, he also felt better informed.

'I do feel guilty about the Contractors,' he said uneasily to Monica. At the back of his mind the compromising photographs of himself and Samantha were nagging relentlessly. He felt hamstrung by them. As the hours passed it became more and more difficult to say anything about them to Monica. The longer he delayed the more guilty he felt. He could not say why, nor could he tell what the loathsome Dandiprat would do if Guy, not he, were to continue with a certain line of enquiry. He would soon find out because it now seemed inevitable that Guy would be arriving at the manor not just with a list of difficult questions but also with a pair of handcuffs. If Dandiprat were to produce the photographs then it would be nothing but malice. They certainly would not prevent Chief Inspector the Earl of Rotherhithe from going about his duty.

'Why do you feel guilty about the Contractors?' Monica wanted to know. 'If they're guilty then they're the only ones who should be feeling guilty.'

'I know, I know,' said Bognor lamely. 'I just find it hard to believe they'd get involved in killing people. Frilly knickers are one thing but murder is a bit different. Orgies...I mean I'd forgive them for organising orgies, even for rich American tourists, but I am inclined to draw the line at murder. I think I might ring them up.'

'With what object in view?'

'I don't know. I just have a hunch.'

'And what form does your hunch take?'

Bognor shrugged. 'I'm not sure. That's the point about hunches. I just have a feeling that while Perry and Sam may be bad they're not wicked. Do you know what I mean?'

Slightly to his surprise his wife nodded.

'I have slightly the same feeling myself,' she said. 'I'll bet they're fully paid up members of Dull Boy Productions but I don't think they'd kill people, not even Brian Wilmslow, who sounds a horror. And certainly not Sir Nimrod, who was rather a dear.'

'But Guy is so ham-fisted, leaden-footed, and pea-brained that he'll accuse them of God knows what and let the real culprit get off scot-free.'

Monica smiled. 'You mustn't let your manifest jealousy of Guy's undoubtedly scrummy appearance get the better of you. He's not as stupid as you think.'

'You mean he's not as stupid as he looks.'

'Husband, dear, you demean yourself. But I'm not going to argue about it. By all means have another go at them if you want. By the way, that stuff about Dandiprat and numismatics. Does Parkinson know anything about coins?'

'I think it's a hobby of his,' said Bognor. 'But I'm never sure. It's coins or stamps or matchboxes. Very boring whichever it is.'

'I have a hunch, too,' said Monica. 'You phone the Contractors. I'm going to see if Bhagwan Josht has a decent dictionary.'

And she loped off mysteriously to the swami and his library, leaving Bognor scratching an ear in some perplexity. He had known his wife for longer than he cared to remember but she was still an astonishing enigma, a constant surprise, and even, when he stopped to think about it, an abiding passion.

Not that this affectionate curiosity about Mrs Bognor interfered with a wide ranging, if lethargic, interest in other women. There was no denying that Bognor was seriously attracted to Samantha Contractor and had been dangerously aroused by her performance in the swimming pool earlier in the day. Phoning the manor at this late hour, when guilt was on the verge of being finally established, was a dangerous and probably unprofessional action. When the chips were down Bognor would have to confess that he was only doing it because he fancied Mrs Contractor enormously and, despite her betrayal this morning, still sensed that this fancying was in some small way reciprocated. A ludicrous conceit when you considered Bognor's

physical appearance but, he told himself, not utterly without justification, he was not without a certain charm. In
his experience there were women, often quite beautiful
ones, who actually preferred the plainer man.

He was greatly relieved therefore when the odious little
butler did not answer the telephone; still more pleased to
hear the breathy, sexy, voice of his fancy woman herself.

'Simon!' she said, gratifyingly. 'Thank heaven you
called. Where have you been? I tried everywhere. I must
talk to you and explain. I've got the film back. You can have
it. But we must talk before it gets any worse. It's urgent.
Where are you?'

'It's not important,' said Bognor, disturbed by the panic
in Samantha's voice. 'Where do you want to meet?'

'Not here,' she said quickly. 'Somewhere safe and anonymous. What about the church?'

'The church?'

'In the village. There'll be no one there. I must talk.'

Bognor frowned. The church sounded a touch melodramatic, but on the other hand it was almost certain to be
empty. And there would be somewhere to sit down. Where
better? The Pickled Herring was out of the question and
he didn't want her coming up to Herring Hall where Monica would be party to the conversation. If Samantha had
really retrieved the film from Dandiprat that particular epi-
sode could be hushed up completely. But he didn't want
Monica to see Samantha handing it to him.

'O.K.,' he said. 'Herring St George church. I can be there
in five minutes.'

'See you there,' said Samantha.

There were those who thought of Bognor as slothful and
indolent, the antithesis of man of action. True, he was by
inclination the apotheosis of armchair man, but when the
need arose he could shift with remarkable speed. It would
be stretching a point to say that he did so with feline grace.
If it was poetry in motion it was pretty blank verse, but
nonetheless effective. It took him under a minute to be at

the wheel of his Mini, heading down the drive and into the sunset.

Monica, hurrying back from the library with the Shorter Oxford Dictionary open at page 452 missed him by a full three minutes. She swore loudly when she realised, then dialled 999 and asked for Guy urgently.

He reached the church in four minutes forty-five seconds and found the scarlet Mercedes parked by the wicket gate. It was a horribly ostentatious car for a clandestine meeting, unlike the anonymous Mini. It was also visible from the windows of the Pickled Herring. He cursed under his breath. Too late now. Better make it quick though. He trotted breathlessly up the path between the yews and tombstones effaced by centuries of English weather, let himself in and stood peering round in the gloom.

'Over here!' she hissed in a church whisper.

She was sitting in the front pew under the pulpit and an ornate, horizontal effigy of a knight in armour – Sir Nymrode Herring who had been one of the few English dead at Agincourt. Bognor went over and sat next to her, inhaling a seductive blast of scent from Jean Patou.

'Here!' she said, and pressed a small saffron Kodachrome roll into his hand. 'And I'm sorry. Will you forgive me?'

Such big eyes, thought Bognor. 'Of course,' he said.

'It wasn't my idea,' she said. 'Nothing ever is and now it's all gone horribly wrong. It was bad enough when they killed that horrible Wilmslow, but Sir Nimrod?' She dabbed at one of her enormous mascara rimmed eyes. 'He was such a poppet.' she said. 'I couldn't believe it. And then I heard they tried to kill you and they'll try again. I told him. I said it was too late and the game was up but he wouldn't listen. He's mad. He thinks he's immortal. He thinks he can get away with anything. I think he's the most evil man I've ever known.'

'What? Perry?!' Bognor was quite shocked. He had expected more loyalty. Besides whatever his shortcomings and misdemeanours Peregrine had always seemed so agreeable. A cad maybe but agreeable. Rather like Nigel Dempster. You disapproved of the deeds but were surprisingly fond of the doer.

'No, you fool, not Perry. Dandiprat!'

'Dandiprat?!'

'Dandiprat.' Samantha seemed exasperated. 'Or Henrici. Or Montano. Or whatever he calls himself.'

'Good grief!' exclaimed Bognor. 'Does he have a naked lady on his bottom?'

It was Samantha's turn to be astonished.

'He what?!' she asked.

'If Dandiprat *is* Henrici and Montano then he has a naked lady tattooed on his bottom.'

'I've never seen his bottom,' said Samantha. 'Thank God, that's one demand he never made.'

Bognor passed a hand over his sweaty forehead and sighed.

'Would you awfully mind beginning at the beginning?' he asked. 'I'm not terribly clever with stream of consciousness confessions. If this is a confession. Is it?'

'I suppose it is,' she said, sadly. 'It's the killing. Neither Perry nor I had anything to do with that. You do believe that, don't you?'

'Just start at the beginning,' said Bognor with a professional detachment he was far from feeling.

'Perry's never been very clever with money,' she said. 'And I suppose I'm an expensive taste. That's where the trouble started. It was when he tried to break into the American market. It seemed to go quite well at first and then, oh, I don't know exactly what happened...Perry got in with a whole lot of rotten eggs. The bills weren't getting paid, and then this man Henrici made a proposition. The FBI were after him and he wanted to disappear. He decided that working as our butler was the perfect cover. Perry would take over the company. The debts would be paid off and...it all seemed quite legal then.'

'Quite legal?' asked Bognor.

'Well *quite* legal,' she said. 'All we were doing was bringing these rich Americans over for a week or so and giving them a good time.'

'Prostitution,' said Bognor. 'Drugs. Obscene literature. Those things Miss Carlsbad writes are disgusting. And the pictures. Even you. Remember I saw one that Damian Macpherson took.'

'I never did pornography,' she said vehemently. 'It was all very tasteful. I always said that. I never posed with anyone or anything else. Just straightforward nudes. There's nothing wrong in that. The human body's very beautiful.'

'And the books were being fiddled,' said Bognor, trying not to be distracted by the beautiful body's tantalising proximity.

'That was all bloody Wilmslow's fault. Then he got greedy. Silly sod.'

'He'd still be alive if he hadn't and no one would be interested in Dull Boy Productions, I suppose.' Bognor shook his head. 'Who exactly killed him?'

'It was Dandiprat and Doc Macpherson. The boys from the Pickled Herring helped carry him into Gallows Wood. Dandiprat and the doctor are the really bad ones. Norman and Felix do as they're told and they've got the wind up at the moment. Miss Carlsbad's just pathetic. And Perry and me...well...I mean we'd never do anything violent. That's why I'm telling you all this.'

Suddenly Bognor froze.

'Shhh!' he said. 'I heard something.'

They sat very still, listening. There was nothing.

'Mouse, probably,' said Samantha. 'But I'd better get back. They'll miss me otherwise. I just want you to remember the one to get is Dandiprat. Without him none of this would ever have happened.'

'Shhh!'

This time there was no mistaking it. Footsteps outside; muffled voices; opening door. Bognor stood, turned, but too late. A diminutive figure in black coat and pin-striped trousers pointed something dull and metallic in their direction. Behind him three other figures could just be made out in the tenebrous dusk.

'Hands above head, Mister Bognor. Also you, please, Mrs Contractor. And don't move at all. Felix, perhaps you'd be good enough to do a quick search. I don't imagine either will be armed but I'd like to be sure.'

'You're crazy, Dandiprat,' said Bognor. 'You'll never get away with this.'

'I've got away with far worse than this in my time, Bognor. And I intend doing so again. And again.' He laughed. 'Question is: how do we dispose of you. As you may have realised I like deaths to look ambiguous. It's a more British way of doing things. Confuses the cops, too. I think in your case a fall from the belfry might be quite neat. It must be about forty foot up. Should do the job nicely.'

Felix advanced on them stealthily. Bognor caught a nasty whiff of rancid eau-de-cologne.

'Don't try anything, Mr Bognor,' he said, beginning to pat Bognor's jacket like a very tentative masseur. 'Mr Dandiprat's gun is loaded and he used to shoot lots of people in the old days back home.'

It was gloomy in the church and Bognor reckoned that there was a sporting chance that Dandiprat would miss. The reverse side of such a sporting chance was that he might very well hit. Bognor was not disposed to take the risk although he had to acknowledge that the spot he was in seemed tightish. He and Samantha – always assuming he could rely on Sam, which was a dubious supposition – were outnumbered four to two and the other team had weaponry. If they wanted to push him off the tower he didn't see how he could prevent them.

Felix continued to pat and prod Bognor in an amateur and hesitant fashion.

'Sir Nimrod left a message,' Bognor called across the aisle. 'It was coded. Naomi gave it to us. The police know who you are. The game is up. Really. There's no point in killing me, however much satisfaction it gives you.'

'All killing gives satisfaction,' Dandiprat replied. 'And yours will give great satisfaction. You've been quite a pain. Also you went to a private school and I can't stand that sort of Englishman.'

'Inverted snobbery...' began Bognor, and then paused. Felix ceased his search and listened too. Far away across the evening air came the unmistakable banshee wail of a police car in full flight.

'Aha!' said Bognor. 'Sounds like the cavalry.'

'Jesus!' said a voice which Bognor identified as Doc Macpherson's. 'They're coming this way.'

'Don't be so dramatic.' Dandiprat was irritated. 'It's just some over-zealous constable chasing after a drunken farm-hand. They won't bother us.'

But the siren was coming closer. And fast.

'Well I'm not hanging around to be caught in flagrante,' said Macpherson.

'Don't move!' snapped Dandiprat. But the doctor obviously did move because there was a sound of footsteps followed by a door being opened. Then there was a crack; a scream followed by prolonged moaning; then another crack; and silence.

'Anybody else who moves gets a dose of the same,' said Dandiprat.

Nobody moved.

The siren was much closer now.

'Don't you think we ought to move?' asked Felix. His voice was unnaturally high-pitched. 'I don't think it would look too good if they found us in here. Especially if you've shot the doctor dead.'

'It's too late now,' said Bognor. 'It makes no odds whether they find you here or anywhere else. You've blown it. The evidence is too conclusive. You've had it no matter what happens.'

Suddenly the door of the vestry to Bognor's right crashed open and the Bengali-Oxford accents of the swami could be heard calling on everyone to put their hands up and their guns down. Seconds later gunfire erupted from both sides of the church. Bognor dived down on to the floor of the pew, pulling Samantha with him.

'I'm frightened,' whimpered Samantha.

'It's all right,' said Bognor, putting a protective arm around her and pulling her to him.

Which was how, a few minutes later, Monica, Mrs Bognor, found them.

'You can come out now,' she said. 'Coast is clear. Guy is here with hordes of fuzz armed to the teeth with stun grenades and Armalites; and the swami's lot have come with an armoury too. I think Guy's turning a blind eye to that. But not, Sammy dear, to you. You, I rather gather, are under arrest for something to do with indecency or running a brothel. Likewise your friend Amanda Mandible – who, according to Guy, was picked up in the middle of a black mass conducted by none other than our very own vicar, the Reverend Branwell Larch. The congregation consisted entirely of American attorneys from Tennessee. Remarkable.'

EIGHT

By the following morning all those in a position to 'sing'
had done so. In every case, like Samantha, they had delivered the simple message that everyone but them was
guilty. Essentially it transpired that the dirty words were
by Miss Carlsbad, and the naughty pictures by Damian
Macpherson of Samantha and other uninhibited ladies
supplied for the most part by Lady Amanda Mandible who
also laid on stately settings for orgies. Rude food was
cooked and presented by the Pickled Herring; grace was
said by the Reverend Branwell Larch; managerial skills,
frilly underwear and 'sexual aids' (including manacles,
whips and face masks) were Peregrine Contractor's
province. He, together with the late Brian Wilmslow, had
cooked the books.

The Pickled Herring boys did grudgingly admit to two
attempts on Simon's life as well as being accessories in the
demise of Wilmslow. The principal culprits, however, were
generally agreed to be Doc Macpherson and Dandiprat.
Macpherson was, in the time honoured phrase, 'dead on
arrival' at Whelk General Hospital. It was agreed that
death was due to shooting by Dandiprat. There were, of
course, witnesses. The doctor was not spoken well of even
in death. He had supplied all drugs, from cannabis to
cocaine and from hash to heroin. He, with Dandiprat,
was unanimously agreed to be the main murderer of
Wilmslow and Sir Nimrod Herring. He would almost
certainly have got life had not Dandiprat given him death
instead.

Dandiprat himself was the most bitter pill. The bogus

butler had done a successful bunk. Somehow, in the confusion, he had managed to escape. Dodging among the gravestones he had reached Samantha's Mercedes unharmed and driven off at breakneck speed in the direction of Whelk. (Like any good butler he always carried a set of his mistress' car keys – just in case.) The Mercedes had been found abandoned on the outskirts of town and there the trail ended. There were regular trains to London and Guy believed he might have caught one of these. Three cars were reported stolen during the night. Any or all of them might have been taken by Dandiprat.

'He won't get far,' averred Chief Inspector the Earl of Rotherhithe next morning at Herring Hall. 'We've put out a red alert at all Channel ports and the international airports. There's a house to house search going on in Whelk as we speak. It's not possible for him to elude the net. This is 1985. You can't just disappear into thin air in 1985.'

'What about Lord Lucan?' asked Bognor mournfully.

'That was years ago,' said Guy. 'This is 1985. Different ball game.'

Talking of ball games, they were walking along the gravel path towards the real tennis court where the swami was to introduce Bognor to the mysteries of that ancient and holy game.

'He's supposed to be a master of disguise,' said Bognor, uncomfortable in a set of whites borrowed from the swami. The swami, though stoutish, was much much shorter than Bognor and the clothes were tight. 'If you ask me he'll surface in Uruguay in a year or two running a rest home for retired Nazis.'

'It's possible,' said Guy seriously, as they entered the tennis court and said good morning to the swami who had just finished an energetic hour with his private professional, a young Australian from Hampton Court. The swami was sweating.

'Stop worrying about Mr Dandiprat,' said the swami.

'He'll turn up, just like any other bad penny ha'penny.' He laughed immoderately for this was a joke. Parkinson had inadvertently triggered the answer to Sir Nimrod's clue. Monica had found the definition of Dandiprat in the dictionary. It was a coin of Henry VII's reign and it was this discovery which had set her charging off with the swami in search of her threatened spouse.

In the event it had proved to be a clue too late but it was gratifying to have solved it at last.

Bognor accepted a racket from the professional as he came off the court and joined the swami who was standing near a line marked five at the service end.

'He's probably hiding in some ditch,' said the swami, beaming up at the high balcony above the wall at the far end. A gaggle of beautiful brides were leaning against the balustrade and watching play. They were all colours and shapes but mostly very beautiful. Bognor noticed Blessed Orchid smiling beatifically at one end of the row.

'Take your eyes off my brides,' said the swami, 'and pay attention. This is the ball. Same size as a lawn tennis ball but underneath the felt it is hard as a cricket ball. Feel.'

Bognor did as he was told, leaned close towards the swami and said, 'Don't look now, but that bride standing on Blessed Orchid's left isn't a bride at all. Unless I'm a swami too it's none other than our friend Dandiprat cleverly made up and wearing a sheet. Perfect disguise.'

The swami was unversed in the ways of the intelligence services, incapable of the cool, implacable response to sudden disaster and dramatic revelation. He looked straight up at the bride on Orchid's left and gasped. 'My God, you're right,' he said. 'It's Dandiprat.'

Dandiprat realised he had been spotted and reached immediately under his robe for the gun which Bognor knew must be there. But the swami was too quick for him. With a lazy graceful swing of the racket he struck the ball high up towards the gallery. Dandiprat was still struggling to extricate the revolver when the ball struck him full in the

187

chest and knocked him to the ground. In seconds Blessed Orchid had the Mafioso butler in a full nelson, and Chief Inspector the Earl of Rotherhithe was mounting the stairs three at a time in order to make the final arrest.

'Good shot, Bhagwan!' said Bognor appreciatively as the audience applauded. 'That's what I call *real* tennis.'